Misfit Lil Robs the Bank

Chap O'Keefe

ROBERT HALE · LONDON

First published in Great Britain 2009

ISBN 978-0-7090-8801-1

Robert Hale Limited
Clerkenwell House
Clerkenwell Green
London EC1R 0HT

www.halebooks.com

rne

1

THE KID AND THE COUGAR

Lilian Goodnight watched him from the cover of the tall timber. He came riding up the trail from town, young, hard-muscled and browned by exposure to sun and wind. Tall, dark, handsome . . . all these desirable attributes. But sitting loose and relaxed in the saddle because he was drunk, or near as damnit.

Not that Miss Goodnight would be one to condemn a body who'd gotten themself booze blind and was maybe a-seeing elephants and a-hearing owls. She was herself permanently in defiance of propriety; was nicknamed Misfit Lil on the strength of it.

She'd watched the fellow before, traversing the ridge close to her lonely shack, on his way back from a ring-tailed tooter in Silver Vein to the bunkhouse of her long-suffering and lately estranged father's Flying G cattle outfit, where he was on the payroll.

His name was Robert M'Cline but Ben Goodnight's hands called him Lucky or just 'the kid'. In the way Lil had of assimilating the country's gossip despite voluntary seclusion, she'd learned the lanky cowboy was out of Texas, fleeing north-west to escape the consequences of a career in minor crime and reckless bravado.

He might have sounded once like someone after her own heart, but that, of course, was committed hopelessly these days to Jackson Farraday. In her favoured men's duds of fringed buckskin coat and pants, Lil strove to emulate the frontiersman. To a tolerable extent she succeeded. She was proficient in many skills like shooting, tracking and trapping that were supposedly the preserve of males, but any ambition to serve the army as a civilian scout, as Jackson did, was plainly as ridiculous as her idolizing of a man twice her age.

Heart otherwise captured, Lil nonetheless took pleasure in observing Lucky M'Cline's regular and careless passing through her lonesome mountain domain and wouldn't want to see any great harm befall him.

And on this occasion exactly that was liable to happen.

The male cougar had been skulking around her retreat for several days. An incompetent hunter had wounded it from considerable range. His rifle's bullet was lodged in its shoulder. Lil had spied on the animal licking the discoloured part with a long pink tongue, irritated by the pain.

The festering wound had plainly slowed the big cat, denying it chances of taking normal prey: nimble deer, mountain sheep and wild goats. With hunger griping its belly, Lil feared it had its predatory amber eyes on Rebel, the trusty grey cow-pony which she kept stabled in the lean-to back of her shack.

But the beast was old and canny as well as vicious. Although it hadn't eaten in days, it fought shy of approaching too closely, of entering the confines of man-made buildings nestled amongst tall cottonwood trees. To wild eyes, the place must look much like a trap, the den of a forbidding, gun-carrying she-human.

Now the smell of horse, and its association with warm meat, was wafting up the open road that soon would wind through the dizzying pass near the seldom-used side-trail leading to her shack.

It was a rare occurrence for a cougar to attack a man on horseback, but it wasn't unknown.

Lucky M'Cline rocked – or maybe it was swayed – happily in the saddle. He mumbled a popular cowboy ballad a mite tunelessly under his breath, slurring many of the words.

'Get six jolly fellers to carry my coffin,
Get six pretty maidens to bear up my pall,
And give to each of them bunches of roses,
That they may not smell me as they go along. . . .'

Left largely to its own devices, his buckskin horse plodded on, following a familiar course to its home corral.

'Had she but told me when she disordered me,
Had she but told me of it at the time,
I might have got salts and pills of white mercury,
But now I'm cut down in the height of my prime. . . .'

Lucky was lost in his rambling thoughts and lulled by his own singing, which to him sounded purely sentimental and melodious. He didn't see stealthy movement atop an overhanging ledge of red rock under which he was about to pass until it was too late.

The buckskin lifted its head and cocked its ears and came to a nervous standstill.

Lucky quit his dreaming, but his wits were too befuddled to take prompt defensive action.

One second he became aware of a sinuous tawny shape above, the long, low body close to the rock. A swishing, four-foot tail was faintly curved near the tip, and a small, powerfully jawed head was thrust ahead of sloping shoulders. The nose was black, shining and all a-twitch.

The next second the cougar was springing at him. When it was already past time to escape its attack, he yanked his shuffling horse into a squealing turn. One hundred and eighty pounds of hissing wildcat landed on his back from the right, hurling him from his seat.

Fortunately, his left foot came free of the stirrup. Sky and earth whirled around him. He hit the ground, rolling. Gritty dust filled his mouth, his nose, his eyes. Either the shock of actually being attacked by a mountain lion or the jarring impact sobered him – rapidly.

His horse was bolting, heading back down trail, bridle and saddle-gear metal jingling. The big cat was on its feet, a scant four or five yards away, gathering itself up to pounce and kill. Lucky struggled to his own and made a frantic grab for his pistol. But the cougar was on him again, bowling him and sending the gun flying, a spinning flash of steel in the last golden light of the sun.

He was fighting for his life, rolling on the ground with the snarling beast on top of him. Though clawed savagely, he strove to grip the beast by the neck with both hands and succeeded. He stared into glowing amber eyes and sweat popped from his brow.

But the squirming cat's muzzle lowered toward him and hideous jaws gaped open, exposing wickedly long, yellow fangs. Fetid breath fanned his face. Raking, hooked claws, unsheathed from hard-padded paws, tore at his clothes and the flesh of his body. A low, throttled growl like the working of machinery sounded from its white ruffled throat.

Lucky knew then the cougar was too big, too powerful, too maddened to be overcome. His hands and arms weakened. He shut his eyes, knowing the deadly jaws weren't to be warded off; were only inches from doing their bloody work. He took a deep breath and waited for the end coming any moment.

But at the last instant, a shot rang out.

The big cougar gave a shrill scream of pain, went limp and fell from him. He scrambled to his feet. The beast was on its back, front paws batting at air. A second shot thudded into its body, and it went still.

He turned to face his rescuer. Though dressed like an old-time mountain man, this was a girl . . . the strange one they called Misfit Lil, who was also the alienated daughter of his big boss, Ben Goodnight, owner of the Flying G. Smoke curled from the muzzle of the drawn Colt hanging in her hand.

'An old tom,' she said, her manner perfunctory as she swaggered up. 'Gone up against the like before, though it's only when they've fallen on ill times they'll pick on a man and his horse.'

'Howdy and thanks. That was good shootin'.' It was scary for him to think about, in fact. 'Hell, supposin' you'd made a mistake, hit me instead!'

She shrugged. 'Small chance of it. I didn't figure to miss and they don't call me the Princess of Pistoleers for nothing. Last Silver Vein gala day, I outshot the best marksman from Fort Dennis.'

'Still, the cougar an' me were movin' targets.'

'So were the crate-loads of empty bottles I smashed in the contest. Every one a bull's-eye. But you're bleeding, feller. Take you to my place for patching up.'

He knew vaguely about the shack she lived in close by, hidden up a side-trail. It had been vacated by an elderly mining engineer who'd retired there with dreams of discovering mineral riches but had been forced to return East by failing health.

They went there directly. It was a one-room cabin of roughly hewn logs with a solid, cast-iron stove and a tin chimney. It struck him straight off that its appointments would have been considered way too primitive for comfort by any ordinary young woman. He was wise enough not to comment.

He said, 'I'm Lucky M'Cline, an' I work for your old man.'

Lil laughed without awkwardness. 'Won't hold that against you. I was working as a 'puncher on a cattle ranch myself till a few weeks back, but I guess I'd gotten bored with High Meadows since the Black Dog business was cleaned up, so I came back here.'

She busied herself collecting a pan of water, clean cloth and a piece of soap.

'Those scratches and abrasions need washing pronto,' she said.

Lucky was rummaging through his memory for all the intriguing scraps he'd heard about her since he'd arrived in this part of Utah.

How 'Miss Lilian' had grown up, motherless and harum-scarum, mixing with the cow-hands on the Flying G. How her despairing father had sent East the complete tomboy she'd become, to a high-toned Boston academy for more fitting education and refinement. How the school had expelled her for ringleading a group of strictly raised but inquisitive young ladies who'd embarked on unmentionable extra-curricular education – unforeseen by their rich parents – with a willing gardener's-boy.

How much later, and dubbed Misfit Lil, she'd paid hard for giving sass to undeserved authority, as was her wont, and suffered no less than a remarkable public spanking by a heavy-handed major from Washington who was later murdered. How she'd taken up residence in this abandoned shack, reluctant to endure the stares of a Silver Vein citizenry she was sure would never forget the viewing of her astonishing correction.

Lucky also thought that close-up the infamous Misfit Lil was most attractive. She had a strong face with clear grey eyes and a resolute chin. More, the athletic body beneath her man's clothing was feminine enough despite its spare trimness. It would have been surely exciting to watch that immodest spanking. . . .

'Stop looking so – *vacant*,' she ordered, as he sat on a hand-made chair with a deerskin bottom, staring at her. 'Take off your shirt. Your pants, too, the left leg's ripped and bloody.'

He felt his face grow hot.

'Well, the shirt mebbe. . . .'

But she was already loosening his belt for him and, as he shrugged out of the shirt, she lifted both his feet and with no ado yanked his Levis down to his boots.

'Hey! What d'you think you're doin'?'

He almost ended up on the stamped-dirt floor, which would have made his embarrassment worse.

'Oh, shush!' she said. 'It ain't the first time I seen a man's legs. 'Sides, this is an emergency. Just think I'm a doctor or a nurse.'

He let her bathe the abrasions, the bruises and several fierce scratches. And she did do it with a kind of professional detachment that, in the event, seemed to border on an insult to his pride. He was more doubtful when she produced a small round tin. Red and gold printing on a worn paper label said it contained a cake of patented carbolic toothpowder, but it was filled with a greasy brown, pungent ointment.

'What the hell's that?'

'Snake dung,' she said, straight-faced; then, when his jaw dropped, she laughed lightly and added, 'No, the stuff's made from mashed woodland roots, herbs, desert flowers and suchlike to an ancient Indian recipe. The army scout Jackson Farraday gave it me. It soothes and heals miraculously. Mr Farraday speaks seven languages and God knows how many Indian lingoes. Not only is he very clever, he's totally trustworthy and a good friend.'

Lucky wondered, how good a friend? Lilian Goodnight, as he'd noted, was attractive. And he happened to have heard Farraday was absent from the Silver Vein country in the Henry Mountains, acting as guide to a scientific expedition, as he did from time to time. Did these circumstances make Lil available and willing to keep other male company? After all, she was living alone and according to his lights there couldn't be much fun in that for anyone, man or woman, however freakish folks might suppose them.

Furthermore, he was growing impatient with his present supposed sweetheart, Virginia Whitpath, a ranch girl always urging him to reform his wild ways and declaring herself unable to accept him on any basis other than church-sanctioned marriage. Maybe dalliance with Lil while Farraday was away would make Virginia jealous enough to change her mind. Anyway, a man was a man, and Lil – reputation and all – had everything it would take to meet the needs of the moment.

Lucky's record showed he set store on living for the moment.

The touch of Lil's strong fingers, gently applying salve to his wounds, served to push his thoughts more temptingly in the direction of better acquaintance. God, they could have a good time getting to know one another properly!

'You're looking pie-eyed again,' she accused. 'Are you still drunk?'

'No, the cougar shook me out of it considerable, I guess.'

He decided honesty, or a modified version of it, might serve his newly formed objectives best. 'I was thinkin' this ain't no place for a young lady to be livin' all by herself.'

'Oh, I can cope all right,' she said airily. 'I was brought up in this country. I know it like the back of my hand.'

'But the dangers—'

She tossed her head. 'Like cougars. . . ? The crew at the Flying G taught me most of what I know about them when I was scarce more'n a button. I remember lying in bed hearing the screams of the big cats fighting for territory in the night. Come spring, they'd be drawn by the scent of fresh afterbirth on the calving grounds. They preyed on the new-borns. The mothers, wicked horns or not, were terrified of the critters. When I got bigger, the men took me hunting them, because they knew I was as good or better a marksman than they were. Believe it – I've hung my fair share of cougar hides on the barn wall to cure.'

It was no tall tale and only confirmed what he'd been told everywhere else. She wasn't bragging. She was a young woman of extraordinary accomplishments, individuality and determination. She broke the mould of convention in a way very few did. Which to him made her all the more an attraction and challenge.

'I was thinkin' more along the lines of lonesomeness,' he ventured. And it was no lie that she struck him as being naturally outgoing and personable, not cut out for the life of a hermit. This close, she was captivating to the point of overpowering.

She said, 'Maybe your notion of a lonely life, unshared, is wrong. It has its compensations. A person can get mighty tired of being gawped at and whispered about by the crowd.'

Thinking fast, Lucky hit on the line to take if he intended to have his chance with Lil.

'You know what I do when I feel that way? To hell with the no-accounts! I get drunk. That or the other when there's new girls at the bordello.'

She raised her eyebrows. 'I might dress like a boy, but I don't think the girls could do much for me, or me for them.'

He laughed. 'Nope, reckon not, so you oughta get drunk. Folks should figure to have a good time. They don't need no finger-pointin'. Mebbe if you was to go inta town partnered it'd be diff'rent. The bigots wouldn't take no notice, or you wouldn't have to notice them.'

'You might be right . . . and I did used to enjoy the top-shelf whiskey they stocked at McHendry's, though my being in a saloon and not a saloon-girl often shocked strangers.'

Lucky spread his arms magnaminously.

'Well, there it is then! You saved my life an' you can come drinkin' with me in town any ol' time you like.'

'Hmm. . . .' Lil said, not quite knowing what she was letting herself in for, 'maybe I could give it a try. I'll ride along when you pass through next pay-day.'

Lil saddled Rebel and went out and rounded up Lucky's runaway buckskin. She caught it easily with the first throw of her rope and brought it back, still a mite skittish, to the shack.

Lucky mounted, they said goodbye and he rode away at a cautious gait. Lil could see it was going to be an uncomfortable journey for him to the Flying G, with every jolting step a hurt to his bruised body. She watched him disappear between the trees. Even after he'd gone, she continued to stare for several moments.

A small smile tugged at her lips. She went back inside, found a match, lighted the lamp, lowered its chimney and trimmed the wick.

Had she done the right thing in accepting the invitation to drink with him in town? At bottom, she wanted only Jackson Farraday when it came to being escorted. Was it fair to lead on Lucky who, she suspected, had ideas that went further than getting themselves drunk?

Still, Jackson had put himself beyond reach; he did that anyway, even when he was around. Maybe Lucky would be a fun substitute. She had no illusions the handsome drifter from Texas would use her for as much and as long as it suited him. And his interest was likely to prove transitory.

Not for the first time, she mused on the inconsistency. Women were deemed necessary to a man's comfort and amusement, but her time's standards embraced the falsehood that respectable women were sexless. Even admission of fantasies was forbidden them.

Lil was still thinking about 'the kid' she'd saved from the cougar when the time came to blow out the lamp and wrap herself in her blankets.

2

KILLING TIME

At the tail end of each week, when cow-hands went to town, Lucky M'Cline and Misfit Lil became a regular twosome at McHendry's, the foremost saloon in Silver Vein. Each with an elbow propped on the mahogany bar top and a foot rested on the brass rail at its front, they'd sip whiskey and swop stories.

The whiskey was none of your rotgut or redeye; was imported, private stock labelled Very Old Scotch Whisky.

The stories from Lucky's side were, Lil suspected, outrageous windies. The shameless Texan's tall tales were of a kind with the as-yet unwritten folklore of the Big Bend country, home of the mythical Pecos Bill, who was said around cowboy camp-fires to have invented, among much else, the first lariat – made up of the tails of ten rattlesnakes tied together tightly.

Sometimes, after Lil and Lucky had taken a few

longer pulls of the strong drink, were feeling good and had run out of tales, they'd go to a corner table and play simple games with cards and dice, or set up a game of checkers. These were noisy with good-humoured taunts and laughter and generally terminated when a card, a die or a checkers piece was 'lost'.

They didn't give a damn about anything and ignored the townsfolks' looks of speculation and of censure at their boisterousness.

One Saturday, when the bottle they slid back and forth between them was near empty and they were exchanging mawkish flattery in the way well-oiled drinking pals will, Lucky said, 'I said it afore, an' I'll say it ag'in, Lil – it was a damn' fine shot when you killed the cougar.'

'Some say you have a certain talent with a gun yourself, Lucky. Were you a gunfighter in Texas?'

'A feller is born with gunspeed or never has it . . . though yeah, guess you c'd call me a middlin' shot.' He blinked around him. 'You want to see?'

'What? Here?'

'Sure. Here.'

'How?'

Lucky's glazed eyes alighted on the saloon's timepiece. Made by the Ansonia Clock Company, of New York and Connecticut, it was some five feet in height with a solid oak case ornamented top and bottom with three fancily turned finials. Below an eighteen-inch dial with Roman numerals, a long pendulum winked in the lamplight as it swung off ponderous seconds in brassy majesty. The pendulum terminated in a shiny disc.

'S-simple,' he said, favouring Lil with his owlish regard. 'See that flashin', tin saucer thing? Waal, I figure it's time time stood still.'

He chuckled at his weak witticism and drew his six-gun. 'You can't!' Lil said, meaning he couldn't do damage to the saloon's ornate clock without a costly reckoning.

Lucky misinterpreted her. Affronted at what he thought was a slight on his ability as a crackshot, he promptly cocked the gun and squeezed the trigger.

The effects of the crash of the gun and the pinging flight of scattered pieces of broken mechanism were instant and extreme. The background buzz of the many conversations abruptly ended, card hands were dropped, a piano stopped playing. Several patrons dived to the sawdusted floor.

The hammerstroke of sound echoed; the fumey smell of powdersmoke spread out across the room.

Then – when it was realized a gun battle wasn't about to erupt – there began the swearing, the ranting and the yelling of abuse.

'What damn' foolishness was that?'

'Yuh could've kilt us, yuh loco kid!'

'Take the gun offa him, somebody!'

Having in her time been involved to later remorse in similar high-spirited stunts, Lil tried to restore calm.

'He meant no harm, guys. Just funning. Look – he's putting the gun back in the holster.'

The bartender wasn't appeased. 'Horseplay or not, that was a hun'erd dollar clock! You gonna pay?'

'My pa'll see you right,' Lil said, though she had no business to make the assumption, which was based solely on having been bailed out of trouble herself on past occasions. 'He'll slap a garnishment on Lucky's wages.'

'How d'yuh mean?' Lucky muttered ferociously. 'Nobody's gonna garnishee my wages.'

'Ain't good enough,' someone else said. 'Call Sheriff Howard!'

At this point Lucky M'Cline, a modicum of better judgement establishing itself, decided it was high time to quit the saloon.

The crowd fell back as he stormed across the room and shoved through the batwings. Lil went in his path, catching them on the return swing.

'Hey, come back! We can't just light a shuck!'

'Ain't stayin' to mess with no tin-badge, gal!' he threw over his shoulder.

'You don't have to fret yourself any 'bout Howard. He's the laziest lawman this side of the Rockies. Wants nothing but the quiet life and a cushion for his fat ass.'

'Mebbe so,' Lucky said. He unhitched his horse from the tie rail outside and swung astride. 'But I ain't stayin' to find out. I'm punchin' the breeze.'

Lil followed his example and mounted her waiting grey.

'No maybe about it – it is so,' she grumbled. 'Jackson says Howard's a stinking, pompous, good-for-nothing jackass. And he's scared. I call him Sheriff *Coward*.'

Sheriff Hamish Howard, Silver Vein's elected peace officer, was an incompetent who largely spent his time collecting taxes – a perk of his office – and buttering-up influential voters. He'd frequently left matters of civilian law enforcement for the army to clean up, earning its exasperation.

Rustlers, horse-thieves, gunrunners, peddlers to Indians of whiskey . . . such frontier scum were allowed to run free in places where Howard had jurisdiction. On occasion, Fort Dennis had been forced to step in, often aided by Jackson Farraday and Misfit Lil.

'Don't care,' Lucky said. 'Mebbe the sheriff has a trigger-happy deputy with an eye on the job.'

Lil laughed sardonically. 'No chance! Deputy Sly Connor toes Howard's line all the way. What's more, I reckon he's secretly plumb scared of women, including me. If he can, he avoids 'em and pretends they don't exist.'

She had little fear of Connor whom she knew to be a slow and unimaginative oaf, always sweaty and pasty-faced.

But they heeled their horses away and left the consternated saloon and the town pell-mell.

'Hell-raisers of a common stripe,' Sheriff Hamish Howard opined to his visitor.

Lieutenant Michael Covington had been asked by Fort Dennis's commanding officer, Colonel Brook Lexborough, to call in at the Silver Vein sheriff's office after his gracious wife, Geraldine Lexborough, had received representations from Miss Purity Wadsworth, full-bottomed president of the Silver Vein Ladies' Temperance Society, and the Reverend Titus Fisher, full-bearded, sniffy sky-pilot of the parish.

'Colonel Lexborough correctly advised Mrs Lexborough that Miss Wadsworth and Mr Fisher's concerns were not a military matter,' Covington said. 'However, the colonel has asked me to pass on our – uh – misgivings. Miss Goodnight is associating with one Robert M'Cline, a rascally Texan of dubious character. I don't need to remind you of her own reputation and record. We see their joint activities as detrimental to public order. There was an incident at McHendry's saloon. Shooting.'

Howard – a big man running to fat, with a small, thin-lipped mouth between flabby jowls – passed his 'hell-raisers' judgement on the pair.

Covington said, 'Then you agree that no good will come of the situation.'

'What can I do?' Howard asked. 'You want I should close the saloon?'

'I know that would be impossible. But perhaps there could be grounds to bar them entry.'

Howard frowned. This sounded like work. He pursed his lips in disapproval of the suggestion and swelled up his chest importantly beneath a tight, conspicuously tin-badged leather vest.

'Connor an' me don't have time to take on no doorman duties at McHendry's.'

The immaculately presented West Point graduate and the slovenly sheriff were plainly unable to come to a meeting of minds, though both had in the past been at the sharp end of Misfit Lil's impudence and suffered the humiliation of seeing her step in to do work that was rightly theirs.

But Covington said, 'Of course, of course. It is your duty to keep the peace, however.'

'Why, sure, Loote'nt, an' thar's letters to be attended to, paperwork to be done, revenues brung in an' sichlike.'

Covington could see most of the papers littering Howard's desk had gathered dust, foodstains and fingerprints during days if not weeks of shuffling. While he did little to further the county's well-being, he was strong in denying or delaying others a say in its running. It wouldn't do to let their energies or initiatives be brought to the notice of the community, even though he was too lazy to show any of his own.

'Of course, Sheriff,' he said again, this time a mite sarcastically. 'I appreciate you're a busy man, but M'Cline is a possible criminal – perhaps you should check whether there's paper out on him. And Ben Goodnight's girl, as we know, is a total disgrace to womanhood.'

This was a line Covington wisely refrained from pursuing. Once he was started, the catalogue of Lil's misdeeds and insults to himself alone would keep him going a half-hour at least. And he wanted to spend no more time in Howard's dreary office. Everything there seemed a turbid, depressing brown, from the out-of-date, light-affected posters and notices on the wall to furniture and fittings coated with the unremoved grime of months of tobacco smoke.

It was a rat's nest. Give him the spartan, scrubbed offices of Fort Dennis's administration block any time:

clean white walls and every paper and document filed in a cabinet or sitting square in a wire basket.

The place smelled, too. Blocked drains? Covington's fastidious nose wrinkled. No, it was coming from the cells.

'Excuse me, Sheriff, don't the slop buckets in your cells need attention?'

'Nossir! They was emptied when the miner Herman was hauled in fer disorderliness. Blind drunk, he were, an' kicked over his bucket. Brown stuff everywhere. Fortunately, his poke was full o' gold dust. I used half his fine to pay some kid to swamp the place out.'

'If you don't mind my saying so, that sounds like scuttlebutt I heard a while back. . . .'

Howard scratched his armpit and crinkled his face in thought. 'Nope. Fifth of March, it were.'

Since it was now July, Covington let the date speak for itself. He flicked a glove at a blowfly and rose.

'Forgive me then for mentioning it. With your valuable time and much else flying by, I won't waste a jot more of it.'

It hadn't been a productive call. Covington, for reasons he wasn't entirely sure of, resented the Lil Goodnight-Lucky M'Cline friendship. He was convinced it was dynamite. They were a pair of prime and primed troublemakers. With the fuse lit, how long to the explosion? And who was going to get hurt? For once, he regretted Jackson Farraday wasn't around. If anyone could talk sense into the pesky girl, it was the experienced scout.

*

Elsewhere, others were also expressing misgivings about Misfit Lil and her new companion. No one in Silver Vein looked upon Lil with more distaste than Miss Purity Wadsworth, a militant spinster and moral zealot in her late thirties.

Virginia Whitpath – much younger, ladylike in her manners and polite – was cornered by Miss Wadsworth between the pungencies of coffee beans and bacon sides in Goldberg's general store, where she was shopping for her rancher uncle and aunt who owned a small property on Silver Vein's outskirts.

'Good day, Miss Whitpath. Have you heard the news? Miss Goodnight's adventurousness becomes wilder and wilder. It's going about she's made a conquest of the young man M'Cline. Wasn't he your beau?'

Virginia's cheeks went red like roses in full bloom. She didn't like Miss Wadsworth's confidential, arch tone, or being reminded that she'd lately lost Lucky M'Cline's affections. The heartache was bad enough; the knowledge that her loss had become a topic of local gossip was worse.

Trying desperately to sound nonchalant, she said, 'Mr M'Cline did take me buggy riding once or twice, and he used to partner me to the town dances and to picnics.'

In truth, she'd liked Lucky's flirting, the touching and the kissing. The boy from Texas was strong and handsome and exciting. She was sure, too, he was experienced in the matter of seeing to girls as they would enjoy being seen to. But in the circumstances in which she lived, with a strict aunt and uncle, she was scared to commit to greater intimacy. Good Anglo-Saxon girls didn't take off their clothes – as Lucky had once asked her – and lie down with men or boys. Only girls in whorehouses did that. Few of those were completely white; many were *mestizo*, Negro, Indian or Chinese. Society had its subtle refinements and requirements which couldn't be questioned . . . except by the likes of a rebel like Misfit Lil.

Just months previously, she'd also been given a memorable lecture about men by her aunt – an unwilling stand-in for a mother who, after her husband's death in a riding fall, had abandoned home and daughter for a drummer based in Chicago. Her aunt's lecture had centred on loss of virginity, the pain of it, the blood and the danger of pregnancy. Short, terse and embarrassing, it had also left her with an abiding feeling that she was dirty and guilty for so much as having thought about Lucky in ways she couldn't help.

Now her own subsequent decision to refuse Lucky's courting until he reformed his reckless ways, becoming a better risk for marriage and the freedom that would permit them, seemed somehow to have rebounded on her.

Miss Wadsworth's eye was as sharp as her malicious tongue and in Virginia's downcast demeanour she saw a chance to stir trouble for Lil Goodnight whom she deplored – but jealously – for her independence, her resourcefulness, her youthful attraction and just about everything else.

'Such a shame,' she tutted. 'Mr M'Cline was your first

suitor, I'll be bound. And the town now has to witness that dreadful Misfit Lil leading him into mischief, addicting him to the demon drink. . . .'

Though Virginia didn't recognize it, Miss Wadsworth's barbs were cleverly designed to reinforce in her impressionable mind the notion that Lucky was really hers and that Lil had stolen him and was the instigator of his waywardness, rather than being a kindred spirit.

The temperance campaigner knew by the time they left the emporium that Virginia, who had all the physical endowments for a full life but no experience of it, thought she was still head and ears in love with Lucky M'Cline and must have him for a husband, even though he was a very unsuitable man for her.

Virginia had been raised to be conventional in her thinking, but she was nonetheless strong-willed. And strong. Miss Wadsworth had successfully provoked her into making up her mind.

She was going 'to have it out' with Misfit Lil!

3

TWO MORE FIGHTING CATS

Two days later the busybody president of the Silver Vein Ladies' Temperance Society sent a small boy with a folded note on crinkle-edged paper smelling of lavender to the Whitpath ranch house. Told it was urgent, he carried out his orders to deliver it personally into the hands of the young lady of the house, Virginia Whitpath.

My dear Miss Whitpath
You may wish to be advised that Miss Lilian Goodnight is presently in town.
Yours very respectfully, Purity Wadsworth.

Virginia gave the boy a quarter, immediately found a

pretext for walking into town, collected her bonnet, shawl and shopping basket and set off.

She had barely arrived in the wide and rutted main street, and was looking about, uncertain where she should present herself, when she saw Misfit Lil leading her grey cow-pony toward the open smithy.

Virginia followed but hung back, summoning her courage and whipping up her righteous indignation.

Lil Goodnight, wearing her men's pants, constituted an unusual sight for a young woman. The pants accentuated her height – she was taller than average – and made her look leggy. But she was not especially threatening or forbidding. Nor could anyone take an instant dislike from her appearance alone. She had clean-looking dark hair, a good profile, a short, straight nose, full lips, and grey eyes. Not a beautiful face, but pretty enough – bright of eye and healthy-looking.

Virginia could understand how she might have caught her Lucky's own twinkling eyes . . . and turned his head.

The sturdy blacksmith was rasping the hoof of a black mare he had snubbed tight by the head to a ring in the wall. He glanced up as Lil and her horse blocked his light from the doorway.

'Howdy,' he said. Then, 'Hold still, yuh ornery minx!'

This bidding wasn't to Lil but to the fidgeting black mare.

'Be with yuh, Miss Lilian, soon as I'm done here,' he continued apologetically. 'Can't be too careful with the crockhead. Kicks like a mockey. Least your'n's got cow sense an' I know I won't git boggered up! Hitch him the other side. Rebel don't never need no chokin' down. Yuh trained him good from a foal. What's his problem?'

'He cast an iron in the mountains, Matt. Near fore. I'll off-saddle and amble.'

Virginia received this information with a modicum of satisfaction and a speeding-up of her pulses. She would have plenty of opportunity to confront Lil while the horse was being attended to by the smith.

She watched quietly but tensely as Lil hefted her saddle over a beam, removed the blanket and hitched her pony to a ring the other side of the forge.

When Lil came out she was ready for her, walking deliberately into her path as she went to cross the street.

'Why, Miss Goodnight!' she said, holding her head high, primly. 'You are just the person I wish to see. I believe you owe me an explanation. Word has it you're leading a young gentleman known to be dear to me into sinful conduct!'

Lil pulled up short, her smooth brow creasing.

'You talking 'bout Lucky M'Cline?'

'The dearest and best of boys, whose friendship you've stolen from me!'

What Virginia saw in Lil's face could have been a glimmering of anger, or the beginning of laughter, suppressed. Either way, she didn't like it. To her, it looked at the moment dangerously like a smirk.

'Might be a hard struggle for your heart to accept,'

Lil said, 'but there was no stealing. Lucky is out for fun of a sort that ain't allowable in your book. So much the better, surely, that you won't be troubled with his demands any more.'

Virginia felt the blood rushing to her cheeks.

'You – you stole him from me!' she charged again.

'Oh, shut up, Virginia,' Lil said in a weary voice. 'Go drag your rope for some other feller.'

That did it. Unable to control herself, Virginia dropped her basket and swung her hand, landing it with crisp slap on Lil's bemused face.

With the faintest of smiles, Lil returned the stinging smack in kind.

'Oh! You shameless wretch!' Virginia said, for a moment stunned by the swift retaliation which filled her eyes with tears of pain and temper. Then all her pent-up fury exploded like a damburst. She threw herself on Lil and bore her to the ground.

However unseemly it might be, Lil responded to her natural instinct to fight back, and she was better dressed for it. She rolled, lithely as a cat, putting herself on top. Virginia, in dress and petticoat, was encumbered by her woman's clothing.

But they were evenly matched physically, being within ten pounds of the same weight, though Lil was a good inch taller.

From the Main Street boardwalk, a man yelled out, 'Fight! Fight!' And fight it was.

Virginia was no weakling and she was spitting mad. She grabbed Lil by the wrists and with a mighty heave tried to toss her off. But Lil's knee slipped between her open legs, trapping her skirt, and when Virginia did succeed in turning her body, it was at the cost of her dress, which tore with a loud ripping sound and peeled right off as the pair rolled again.

A crowd of cheering onlookers, mostly male, had quickly gathered, to egg the combatants on.

'Go it, gals!'

'Scratch her eyes out!'

'Hold her down!'

Nothing was to be lost now except the fight. Undeterred by the removal of her dress or the fear of making a greater spectacle of herself, Virginia was first to jump to her feet, leaving Lil pinning only a shucked, dusty and once pretty frock.

'God, you're slippery as a snake!' Lil said.

Virginia swung her daintily booted foot hard at Lil's head.

But Lil was fast and had learned the tricks of rough and tumble early in life, observing the occasional wrestling contests between the hands at the Flying G. Rising to her knees, she clung to the swinging leg.

'No, you don't!'

Toppling, Virginia grabbed Lil's hair and tried to pull her head back, forcing the fingers of her other hand into Lil's open mouth as she spoke. Lil promptly bit the fingers.

'Bitch!' Virginia cried.

Amid more screams and howls, the girls collapsed to the dirt again. The battle was fast and soon had them threshing around, raising clouds of gritty dust. Whenever they became temporarily locked together and their struggles paused, imaginative advice was hurled at them as to exactly how and where they should squeeze and poke.

'Don't you dare!' Virginia blurted, fearing the ruin of her delicate integrity.

Thankfully, Lil didn't oblige the crowd. She had Virginia in a backhold, her hands and arms were fully engaged, and she was bearing her full, immobile weight. She had neither capability nor intention to turn self-defence into invasive assault.

In fact, Lil relented at a stage when she had Virginia doubled up in another crushing hold and the ranch-girl's submission to a merciful opponent might have been a wise option.

But when she was released, Virginia promptly resumed swinging punches.

Lil, still rising, got a fresh lock on her right leg, this time higher up. They both ended up on the ground once more, head to tail, and Lil exerted leverage.

The excited spectators were hooting in a frenzy of ribald enjoyment.

'Keep goin', Ginny – you're showin' out jest dandy!'

'You can lick her, Lil!'

'Ain't this a fine ol' game!'

Virginia realized she was coming off the worst. The girl raised on the Flying G was exceptionally tough and wiry. Also, she had more experience of this sort of thing.

'Oh, you horrid beast!' she screamed at Lil.

The crowd of fascinated cowboys and miners shouted more encouragement, the gist being they'd be content only when Virginia was thoroughly trounced and paying with the loss of all her former airs and pretensions.

'Let's see her beaten proper!'

'Naw – *improper*!'

All the while, more people were coming out from Silver Vein's shops and businesses to see what the fuss was about.

The Reverend Titus Fisher hurried down from the parsonage beside the white clapboard church at the town's edge and stayed to watch, absorbed.

'Well I never, well I never,' he kept saying . . . till he was given a strange look by a church-going matron. He coughed, racked his brains for suitable scripture and came up with the verses:

'I will, therefore, that men pray everywhere, lifting up holy hands, without wrath and doubting. . . . In like manner also, that women adorn themselves in modest apparel, with shamefacedness and sobriety. . . . with good works!'

For all that, he kept his gaze fixed on the two panting and straining female wrestlers, one who had the temerity to dress as a man and the other a miss, formerly of unblemished reputation, who fought in a state precariously close to nature.

'It's not my fault,' Lil said. 'Do you surrender?'

'No I do not!' Virginia cried in frustration, and bunching her hands into fists hammered furiously at Lil's bottom.

'All right then! You asked for it!'

Lil was very strong. She planted her shoulder into the top of Virginia's soft right thigh, clung on to the seized leg, and lurched to her feet.

Virginia found herself being carried upside down, head and arms dangling.

'Let me down, Lil Goodnight!' she screeched. 'My uncle and aunt will kill you for this!'

She didn't really think so, but she was increasingly alarmed her strict guardians might kill her when they learned of her exposure in her underwear. The horror! The shame!

She screamed and pummelled at Lil's hard legs frantically.

'You need to cool off!' Lil said.

And she staggered across to the forge and tipped Virginia into the big, open butt of water that Matt used in the course of his blacksmithing.

'Omigod. . . !' Virginia said, but the shriek ended in a gurgle as her head went under the dark, oily surface.

She struggled to stand up, shaking long strands of soaked hair, shivering and choking up swallowed water.

The crowd clapped and cheered ever more enthusiastically.

Looking down, Virginia realized her fine crepe chemise and her cotton drawers were near transparent.

With a cry of distress, she ducked down again into the dirty water till only her head and the top of her shoulders were above the surface.

Bellows of raucous laughter mocked her. The citizens of Silver Vein had never enjoyed such indecorous merriment created in their town.

'Well I never!' the Reverend Fisher said.

Lil took pity on her and borrowed a spare but smelly

horse blanket from Matt. She handed it to her without a word, tutted, swung on her heel and strode off, casting black looks at the disappointed voyeurs, who were begging her to stay and 'do' the vulnerable Virginia in further, abusive ways.

What some men expected was contemptible, Lil thought. It made her furious inside to hear the crude way they talked about her tussle with Virginia. Losing a fight was one thing, but as she knew from past experience it was another – altogether different – to be exposed and ridiculed for the benefit of an audience.

Nor would she find any pleasure in further humiliating the irritating girl she'd fought and beaten. She'd no wish to seal domination by inflicting any of the imaginative punishments recommended.

Enough that Virginia's basket, bonnet, shawl, torn dress and demure reputation already lay crushed and trampled in the rutted dust. . . .

Girl-on-girl fights were not unknown in frontier communities. Though they were vastly outnumbered by fights between men and boys, it had also to be allowed that in most territories males outnumbered females eight to one. And life for women was drear and hard. Drudgery and hardship was the lot of many; hardship eventually begat hardness; the small pleasures and luxuries of life were come by infrequently, which fed competition, bitterness, hatreds.

Small towns and isolated ranch houses were claustrophobic places despite the West's wide open spaces, of which the majority of women saw little more than what lay frustratingly beyond the view from their windows. No wonder jealousies and rivalries sometimes boiled over. Men, of course, were not in short supply, but even in whorehouses the ladies were known to fight over a desirable man with a habit for making gifts as well as payment.

It was, however, unusual for a fight between young women to take place publicly, on a main street.

Miss Purity Wadsworth watched the clash between Virginia and Lil discreetly from behind the cover of a hay wagon. On the fight's outbreak, the wagon had been most conveniently deserted outside the livery barn by the workers about to unload it.

She was not pleased to witness the Reverend Fisher shoulder through to the front row of the mob. Curse it, he looked like he was ogling. . . ! Well, what could one expect? At bottom, a man of the cloth was just a fool man. Men should be routinely gelded – only chosen specimens left as entires, for breeding purposes.

She was bitterly disappointed that Virginia, a well-built and healthy ranch-girl, didn't prove a match for the lithe and speedy Misfit Lil, whom she regarded as an abomination with her men's clothing, her drinking, and – worst of all – her unorthodox, outspoken thinking.

She gnashed her teeth in quiet rage when the satisfying anticipation of witnessing Lil's humbling came to nothing. She groaned when at last order was restored and Virginia hobbled away huddled in a blanket for modesty and Lil walked off, head high, an air of assurance about her.

But all Miss Wadsworth's hopes were not dashed.

For she had a back-up plan. Lilian Goodnight would get her comeuppance!

4

VENGEANCE FOR VIRGINIA?

Miss Wadsworth was an avid reader of newspapers, in which it was her wont to find much to deplore, especially in the reports of crimes and court proceedings where she could monitor 'the rising tide of moral perversion'.

It was from the newspapers that she had learned about Dr François Guiscard. In the course of a lecture tour, the French doctor was due to speak in Green River, a nearby railroad town run by the Denver & Rio Grande Western Railway.

The curious citizens of Green River will be enlightened by the good doctor's revelations, which will de-mystify for them the sciences of mesmerism and hypnotism, one report said.

Dr Guiscard has graciously accepted an invitation to describe for the education of the general public his manifold successes in these fields, for which he predicts exciting expansion in the Americas. In particular, Dr Guiscard was responsible for the treatment and cure of insane and delinquent women at the famous Paris hospital, La Salpêtrière, under the supervision of Professor Jean-Martin Charcot, a researcher in nervous-system disorders. . . .

The phrase 'delinquent women' immediately caught Miss Wadsworth's beady eyes. A most suitable candidate for inclusion in that class was Misfit Lil!

A bell also rang in her mind concerning the details of Lilian Goodnight's misdemeanours in Boston, at the finishing school for the adolescent daughters of good family. Her excellent memory for impure details told her that one of the other girls, corrupted by and expelled from the academy at the same time as Lil, had been sent to the Massachusetts State Lunatic Hospital at Taunton, suffering 'venereal feelings from excitement'. And here, in the newspaper item, it was also recorded that during a short tenure at the very same institution, Dr Guiscard had corrected young women's 'hysteria' through the medium of hypnosis.

It had to be a sign from Above, Miss Wadsworth decided.

She extended her investigations by buying, at expense she hoped would be justified, every Eastern newspaper she could find in Silver Vein. Some were months old.

She further learned, from insinuations in a critical editorial in one of the papers, that Guiscard had departed Massachusetts for the West suddenly. The leader writer hinted at irregularities in his practices and threw doubt on 'le magnetisme animal', or mesmerism, which was at the heart of his regimens.

Let the good doctor transport these outmoded prescriptions to the new territories, though we venture to suggest that the brave frontier folk would better benefit from improvements in diet, sanitation and midwifery.

The suggestion was that Dr Guiscard had come under a cloud and was heading for less regulated parts where his lectures and charlatanry would meet fewer questions. Miss Wadsworth did not consider this such a bad thing – she suspected as a consequence of such discrediting he might well be available to co-operate in a certain scheme she hoped could be put to him.

The next day, she went calling at the Whitpath ranch, ostensibly to enquire after the health of young Miss Virginia following her shameful ducking.

'I saw it,' she told Virginia's uncle, George Whitpath. 'So cruel, and all the fault and work of that monstrous Lilian Goodnight! Something must be done.'

'But what, ma'am?' Whitpath asked. 'It be most dejecting work, being the guardian of a young lady about grown. Ben Goodnight with all his money tried to send his'un away, and what good did it do? She come back, and now she's gotten into tarring a prop'ly brung-up girl with the same brush.'

'Given Mr Goodnight's vexation, Mr Whitpath, and certain information I have come across, I do believe we can arrange a favourable solution and Virginia will have her revenge. Perhaps you would be so good as to let me speak to her in private.'

The Whitpath house was on two levels and Virginia

was in her small bedroom, either banished there by her aunt to do penance or to recover from her ordeal. Miss Wadsworth judged she was suffering from a chill or shock.

She was sitting in bed, a pillow behind her back against the hard iron frame at its head. Her face was pale. The windows were shut and the room was sultry with a cheap, floral perfume. An unemptied chamber pot, though discreetly pushed under the bed, didn't improve the air.

Miss Wadsworth said, 'You have my fullest sympathy and support, Virginia – I may call you Virginia, mayn't I? We must see to it that the dreadful Goodnight girl does not go unpunished.'

Virginia shook her head sadly. 'Once, I guess her pa would have attended to that, as my uncle has, but unlike me Lil has struck out by herself.'

'Ah, and there you've put your finger on it, Virginia. Mr Goodnight must be persuaded to take his erring daughter in hand and see that she is taught the error of her ways.'

'But he already tried, Miss Wadsworth. He sent her to Boston at considerable expense, and it didn't work.'

'Because he sent her to the wrong people, Virginia.'

Virginia, if foolish in some respects, was intelligent enough to realize that Miss Wadsworth was aching to pass on information she considered important.

'There're right people for correcting a Misfit Lil?'

'Well, a person, I believe – a French doctor called François Guiscard. And he's here in America, very close at hand in fact. I'm sure he could be persuaded to take on the case of Miss Lilian Goodnight for an appropriate – uh – consideration.'

Virginia was still puzzled. Her first question was, 'What would this doctor do?'

Miss Wadsworth told her about La Salpêtrière and what she'd discovered of its unlovely history, accommodating the female mad and indigent.

'The hospital once treated the problem of Paris prostitutes, who'd been committed as its patients, by pairing them with convicts and deporting them to Louisiana, which had to be peopled and needed women. It struck me that an important doctor previously associated with such an establishment could think up some similarly appropriate way of treating a Misfit Lil, who is, after all, plainly touched in the head.'

For the first time in days, Virginia's heart leaped and her spirits lifted. Could a fate like that of the Paris unfortunates be dealt to her rival for Lucky's affections?

'Oh, how wonderful that would be!' she said, her glee as transparent as it was malicious. 'Lilian Goodnight cured of her tricks – reformed, perhaps as an obedient wife to some low ruffian from a penitentiary. And sent to some far-off outpost to be made with child!'

Miss Wadsworth hid her smile. Despite her trouncing by Lil, Virginia was still a force to be reckoned with. She'd cottoned to the notion of destroying her enemy with enthusiasm. The girl clearly hated Lil and was determined to have vengeance against her.

'Indeed, think of it! Such would be a sweet, sweet victory,' Miss Wadsworth said. 'You – we – must never give in until Miss Goodnight's pernicious influence on Silver Vein, misleading men like Lucky M'Cline, is removed. I do believe the stakes are higher than they have ever been. . . .'

'Yes, you're right, Miss Wadsworth. Very high. Lil must be made to pay for all the wickedness she has done. But how will she be delivered into this Dr Guiscard's care? Who will arrange it? How will the doctor's bills be paid? I have no money, and my uncle and aunt wouldn't want to spend theirs.'

Miss Wadsworth smiled wryly and produced what she thought was the masterstroke of her scheme.

'Why, Mr Ben Goodnight will pay, of course. Isn't the Flying G the richest cattle outfit in this country, and hasn't he long been vexed by the problem of his rebellious daughter? The proposition needs only to be put to him independently and innocently and I believe his co-operation will be forthcoming. Perhaps your uncle and your charming self, as one of his daughter's peers, would be the best candidates to bring the matter to his attention?'

Virginia was not convinced entirely that her uncle and herself were the best persons to make the representations, but she did want Miss Wadsworth's promising plan to work. She recognized, too – as Miss Wadsworth doubtless had – that the president of the Silver Vein Ladies' Temperance Society was not the best choice either. Mr Goodnight would smell skunk, sure as tooting.

The rich cattleman didn't have much to do with town gossip, and probably regarded Miss Wadsworth as a meddling do-gooder. Many secretly did. He'd know Miss Wadsworth would be the last to have Lil's interests at heart, and any declaration that she was acting out of good intentions would instantly make him wary. But he could scarcely deny his errant child's black reputation.

Virginia said, 'Hmm. . . .' thoughtfully. 'I don't know whether I'm qualified for the task, Miss Wadsworth, but I'd be willing to try if you can also persuade my aunt and uncle that I have the duty.'

'That's it, young lady. Tenacity will pay, providing your revenge, I'm sure.'

But Miss Wadsworth's confident assurance was to prove less of a factor than other developments outside her oversight.

Misfit Lil was considerably less exercised by the outcomes of the fight on Main Street than her erstwhile opponent. She wanted Lucky M'Cline for fun. She didn't have the serious designs of a long-term union based on legal marriage that motivated Virginia. Consequently, she worried more about Lucky's mercurial and unpredictable temper than his pathetic ex-sweetheart's pique.

It was his volatility, she believed, that had led to the unfortunate episode with the saloon clock. But even with that matter patched over by a promise of compensation from the Flying G, Lil feared worse could follow.

For instance, besides his dislike of authority, Lucky was imbued with an unreasoning hatred of black people and men in blue uniform. This was brought to a head when a detachment of troopers from a black regiment was posted to Fort Dennis. The men were allowed to spend off-duty time in town. Some frequented McHendry's saloon, to which Lucky took exception.

'Buffalo soldiers!' he complained to Lil. 'That's what the Injuns call 'em on account of their hair. They ain't needed in our saloon an' should stay clear.'

Lil sighed. 'Why do you say a thing like that? My friend Jackson Farraday says the army here appreciates their help. Their regiments have fought against hostile Indians of many tribes. They were in campaigns against the Apache chiefs Victorio and Nana – campaigns actually more important than the ones against Geronimo. And they've cleaned up Mexican outlaws and Border desperadoes.'

Lucky was unconvinced.

'But the Negroes were on the side of the Unionists in the War Between the States. They weren't comin' to the aid of beleaguered white troops then. They were killin' good Confederate boys. In Texas I got older kin an' such who've told me 'bout their dirty ways.'

'They look just as clean and inoffensive as white soldiers to me,' Lil said. 'Anyway, folks figure to have a good time in a saloon. They don't need trouble.'

But Lucky kept hunting it.

The soldiers were playing cards and one of them had won a big pot.

'I'm putting up drinks for everybody,' he said. 'Come on, fellers, up to the bar. All drinks are on me. Set 'em up, barkeep!'

Chairs were pushed back, scraping fresh tracks in the sawdusted floor. Uniformed men, ranch-hands and miners tramped up to claim their free drink.

Lucky stayed firmly put, aloof from the comradeship of the offer. The soldier celebrating with his winnings noticed.

'You're not going to drink with us?' he asked pleasantly.

Lucky waved Lil's bottle of real Scotch whisky. 'I gotta drink! Real likker all th' way acrost th' ocean an' costin' twenty-five dollars the bottle. Don't need none o' your rotgut. Shove it between your own lips.'

Smacking his own, he refilled his and Lil's tumblers.

The soldier shrugged. 'I meant no offence, sir, but suit yourself. Buy your own drinks if you prefer it that way and don't like our company.'

His polite, well-spoken manner inflamed Lucky, who was half-drunk.

'Don't take that high-falutin' tone with me, black man!' he said loudly.

The hubbub of the crowd ceased and a sudden hush fell over the room. The soldier and Lucky were glaring at one another, Lucky with bloodshot eyes, the soldier stiff with wounded pride.

'Easy, Lucky,' Lil said. 'That's no way to talk.'

The soldier was reassured by the man's strange girl companion taking his side.

'In point of fact,' he said, 'your friend is being grossly insulting. Maybe he should apologize, if the words don't get stuck in his craw.'

Lucky stared at the soldier in astonished disbelief.

This man, this Negro in a blue uniform, was asking for an apology! Speechless, he let out a squawk of rage before – to Lil's dismay – his hand left his glass and clawed for his gun.

The best Lil could do was knock his arm. Even so, the gun went off with its brief, stunning thunder . . . and the shot that had been aimed at the soldier's midriff ripped through his right sleeve, high up.

Pandemonium broke out as the saloon's patrons hastened to get clear of the party of soldiers. Those nearest the door swiftly ducked out.

'Send for the sheriff!' the barkeeper yelled.

The wounded soldier clutched his arm where blood started to appear.

'Git out, yuh scum!' Lucky screamed. He waved his six-gun at the three other soldiers. A thin coil of smoke from its muzzle traced a wavering path through the poisoned air between them. 'Pull stakes afore I kill yuh!'

'Lucky, don't do this!' Lil implored.

But it was too late for appeals to reason.

The soldiers were three experienced fighting men; a gun had been drawn on them and they were being threatened by just one. While he might shoot one more man, the other two would shoot him.

They went for their army pistols.

5

WARRANT FOR LIL

Lil swore and shoved the drunken Lucky aside with a sideways thrust of her hip. Her hands dropped simultaneously to the use-darkened butts of the twin Colts holstered at her waist. She whipped them out with eye-baffling quickness.

'Hold it!' she snapped at the buffalo soldiers. 'That's enough bloodshed over some loose mouth.'

'Damn yuh, gal!' one of the soldiers said. 'The blowhard done shot Abraham!'

Lil saw the speaker's finger beginning to tighten on the trigger. She made a split-second decision. She fired as he fired. Lead smashed into the wall over her and Lucky's heads. But the soldier wouldn't be firing again quickly. The gun was plucked from his nerveless hand by Lil's amazingly accurate shooting and he clutched a maybe broken wrist.

'Next time I shoot to kill!' she told the others.

Meanwhile, blood was welling through the sleeve of Lucky's undeserving victim, from the hole in his upper arm that the bullet had made. It was bright red blood, glistening, coming in small spurts.

'Take your Abraham to the doc's,' Lil suggested. 'Come on, Lucky – you've gotten us in a mess again. It's time we lit another shuck!'

The pair made it out to their horses. Lucky was quieter now, seeming bemused by the exchange of gunfire. He made two tries at settling a boot in the stirrup before he succeeded. He pulled himself into the saddle, lurching, and Lil hit his horse on the rump. They clattered out of town.

No one pursued them.

Outside the limits, in gathering darkness, the cool air rapidly cleared Lucky's head and they rode abreast wherever the terrain allowed it, so they could talk.

'Where do we go?' he asked.

'No more lifting the bottle tonight, so you'll be headed for the Flying G, I reckon.'

Lucky pondered this.

'Can't,' he said at length, unburdening himself. 'The damn clock . . . your pa said I had one last chance after that. Any more trouble an' I'd be rollin' my blankets.'

'Guess you'll be drifting then. You must still have some friends back in Texas.'

As she said it, Lil realized she'd miss the bothersome rogue, despite his volatile temper and hidebound beliefs.

Lucky said, 'Texas is a far piece. Mebbe I could spend some time at your cabin.'

Lil swallowed, made a spur-of-the-moment decision she knew in her heart carried unspoken implications, and said, 'All right then.'

After this latest ruckus, Lucky might need protection from the law. She might need it herself. It hinged on whether Sheriff Hamish Howard would be stirred into action.

For the first time in a long spell Lil felt a certain anticipatory excitement. Under an emergent sprinkling of stars, they plodded toward whatever prospects awaited in sharing the hermit's shack Lil had made, and previously guarded, as a personal sanctuary.

Lieutenant Michael Covington's worst prognostications for the M'Cline–Misfit Lil alliance had come about. The dynamite had exploded – right in the army's own face – with the shooting at McHendry's saloon.

Another visit with Sheriff Hamish Howard in his depressing office was top of the order of the day.

'What do you intend to do this time, Sheriff?' Covington asked. 'Better than nothing, I hope. It's more than a matter of a damaged clock now. Troopers have been shot and wounded. That can't be ignored. The military will demand an outcome.'

Howard spread his hands helplessly.

'You people swear the warrants out, then I guess I hafta serve 'em.'

'Precisely, sir! That's what you're paid to do. And you can take it as read that the warrants will be forthcoming in short order – from Colonel Brook Lexborough himself if not higher.'

'Me an' Deputy Connor'll need time to raise a posse,' Howard prevaricated. 'Ain't no simple breach o' the peace, an' that Lil is hell on wheels with a pistol, yuh know that. Folks mightn't be willin'—'

'Don't let them refuse,' Covington snapped back. 'The law backs its peace officers. It gives you the right to deputize citizens to carry out arrest duties. Remind them it's an offence to refuse to join a posse. I want to see M'Cline and Lilian Goodnight in your jail!'

He could have added that he contemplated the prospect of Misfit Lil languishing with her new Texan pal in Howard's stinking cells with satisfaction. Maybe it would take the sharpness out of her tongue; make her more respectful. It couldn't happen soon enough.

Howard thought the unwelcome task through.

'Guess they'll be at that ol' shack. Mebbe we'll hit 'em at dawn. Catch 'em when they're apt to've gotten drowsy an' tuckered out at the tail end of the night. M'Cline's a hungry rooster an' Misfit Lil's no more'n a slut. Fact, it'd boost posse volunteers if it were put about thar'd likely be sport left over fer them with the bitch. . . .'

Covington said stiffly, 'Good strategy, Sheriff. See that it's done.'

But his mouth had gone dry and the words came in a rasp. Which was ridiculous. He didn't care what happened to Lilian Goodnight. She was no lady. She'd always made insultingly plain her dislike of him and the standards he upheld. She purported to care only for Jackson Farraday. But Farraday was many years her senior, and would never take advantage of her unstinting admiration. Farraday considered he, Covington, would make Goodnight an ideal, complementary partner in his stead. How nonsensical that was!

And yet for some reason Covington's stomach churned to think of the exasperating, sassy Misfit Lil being dragged from a bed before sunrise and pawed by a bunch of roughnecks.

Lil had spent two nights and one day living with the consequences of her consent to shelter Lucky. Nothing had happened to her that she hadn't really wanted to happen; that hadn't happened before. Nothing bad.

Lucky, long teased by Virginia, was enthusiastic and appreciative. And he was no slouch when it came to fulfilling neglected needs. Some men were good like that, finding the glow, building it into a fire.

But he was not her 'man for life', and she entertained no illusions or regrets on this score. Lil often wondered how many decades would pass before white women could all be as the Hopi Pueblo Indian women had been before the Conquest and the coming to America of the Spanish friars. The Pueblos had been joyously free of taught inhibitions; saw no shame in what instinct and inclination told them to do.

The main comfort in the long-gone mining engineer's primitive home was its bed. Barely wide enough for two, it had served. They were sleeping just before dawn on the second day when Lil became aware of approaching horsemen; the muffled pound of hoofbeats on the hard-packed trail, and then the rustle among fallen leaves and dry grass under the trees around the shack.

She nudged Lucky awake instantly and sat up, sweeping the blankets off them.

'Company!' she hissed. 'Out among the trees, sneaking up on us, I figure, and none too smart about it either.'

'The law prob'ly,' Lucky said bitterly. He reached hurriedly for his clothes and stepped into his pants. 'I ain't goin' peaceable. There'll be a shootout!'

Lil sighed.

'You'll be pushing your luck, Lucky. They'll have the numbers. It's no situation for gunfighting skills.'

Lucky was incredulous. 'You want I should surrender?'

'I've been thinking about it. Giving ourselves up could be for the best. No one died. Maybe a judge will let us off with a fine and payment of damages.'

'More likely I'll get two years on a chain gang!'

From outside, a voice called out.

'M'Cline! We know you're holed up in thar. Come on out with your hands up!'

Lil said, 'That's Sheriff Howard. You going out?'

Lucky's eyes flared. 'Like hell I am!'

Without stopping to think, he snatched up his Colt, crossed to the window, pushed open the shutters and snapped off two blind shots.

'That's my answer!'

It brought an immediate response. A hail of lead came through. Lucky ducked down and pulled back only a split-second in time to avoid instant death.

The possemen carried on firing for what seemed an age but was probably less than a minute. An unlit lamp was smashed to smithereens, pots and pans on a high shelf facing the window were dislodged, bent and buckled. A bullet bounced off the stove chimney with a ringing boom. Everywhere, holes and splintery cracks appeared as lead burrowed into the cabin's timbers.

Bits of debris flew, although none hurt Lil or Lucky.

'You fool, Lucky!' Lil said. Her face, which had still been prettily flushed one side from the warmth of the bed's pillow, visibly paled in the half-light. 'How could you do such a stupid thing? Do you want to make yourself an outlaw? Ruin your life?'

Howard hollered out a second time.

'You an' your whore wanna die in thar, kid? We give yuh one more chance—'

But Lucky didn't want to know about the sheriff's chance. He bobbed up again, fired again. And it was more of the same. The posse's guns poured in more screaming slugs that sliced the air inches above their lowered heads.

A splinter cut stingingly into Lil's bare shoulder but did her no incapacitating harm.

'It's no good, Lucky,' she said. 'We have to give in.'

He said, 'The shootin's started. Nothin' will stop it till we're outa here or cut to doll rags.'

Another tense lull settled around them.

Lil gave the tight fix they were in some more frantic thought. Their tails were surely in a crack. She concluded the most desperate of measures was necessary and becoming vital.

'We can still surrender,' she repeated.

'No way. I show myself now an' they'll blast me down straight off.'

Lil said simply, 'Then I must show myself.'

6

NEGOTIATING TACTICS

'*You*? You're crazy, Lil! That'd equally be suicide.'

'I don't think so. They won't have the gall to shoot down a defenceless, harmless girl, will they?'

'They surely won't know that. You're Misfit Lil, the Princess of Pistoleers, remember? The yeller-gutted bastards'll be too yeller *not* to shoot.'

'The way I figure to go out they'll know I've got no guns – that I'm no threat. They won't help but see it, less'n they're blind, which they ain't. And while they're still staring, I'll tell 'em we're quitting, giving ourselves up for fair trial.'

'What are you babblin' about, gal? They'll shoot first, ask questions never.'

'Don't you believe it, Lucky. Trust me – I know what will stop these galoots in their tracks. Fact, I can't think of anything else that will do the trick near as well.'

Lucky, poor boy, might know a tolerable lot about pleasing women, but he'd forgotten his fellow-men responded to the same stimuli as he did, albeit not all as gratifyingly. In the stress of the moment, he seemed to be overlooking she'd not dressed and was as entirely naked as when she'd risen from the bed. She didn't intend to change that, though he might be assuming she did.

Before he could argue, she said, 'I'm going out – right now!'

Lucky realized at the last moment exactly what she had in mind.

'Hey! Come back!' he cried. 'Those wolves'll eat you!'

But in three flashing, long-legged strides she was to the door and going through into the open.

Her bare flesh crawled as she thought how her optimistic guesses might be all wrong, how that same flesh might be about to be peppered with bullets from a firing squad of flaming gun muzzles. But it didn't happen.

Instead, her startling appearance was received as she'd hoped – with a chorus of gasps from men who seldom saw much more than an ankle except in the marital bedroom or the whorehouse. This was followed by a mixture of nervous guffaws first, then appreciative growls.

'Don't shoot, fellers! I'm innocent—' Realizing that sounded ridiculous, she broke off, gulping, and continued, 'No more threat than a new-born. I've come out to say you can arrest us. Anything was better than cowering in there waiting to die.'

Eyes popping, Sheriff Howard managed to keep his head.

'Stay right thar, Lil Goodnight! Keep your guns cocked, ever'body else. This might be a trick. We know yuh ain't got nothin' up no sleeves, gal, but that ain't lettin' yuh off no hook. Not till M'Cline throws out his guns an' shows his face, mitts grabbin' fer the sky.'

Lil said, 'You can rest assured it's no trick, Sheriff. I didn't want this gun battle to take any lives, is all.'

She tried to sound even and composed – but it was hard to pretend she was in a position to negotiate terms, wearing not a stitch of clothing. It was one of the biggest tests of self-confidence and daring she'd set herself. Could she pull it off?

'Let Lucky come out without any shooting and we'll come quietly.'

'By God, yuh'll come quietly, yuh trollop,' Howard agreed. 'Yuh don't, an' M'Cline dies an' yuh hafta take whatever the men figger yuh've got comin'.'

Lil scanned the faces of the bunch. In the dim light, all except the few like Deputy Sly Connor, who evidently couldn't get over his embarrassment, were feasting their eyes on her. She heard muttered comments that weren't reassuring.

'Ain't it a temptation?' one said in gravelly tones, and she could almost see the beads of perspiration she imagined were on his brow.

She felt terrible, wanted to put out their lamps, but she was determined to hold her ground and not let show how uneasy she was.

Stretching a point, she called out, 'Lucky, the Sheriff says there won't be any more shooting. Throw out your guns, come out docile-like and I'll be safe, too.'

She *hoped* she'd be safe. . . . Involuntarily, she found herself assessing her chances if this didn't work out and the worst befell.

In the cabin, Lucky cursed. 'Are you sure? Sounds like they got their dander up.'

' 'Course I'm sure. It's the only way.' But she added quietly, to herself, that danders were the least of her worries.

After some more agitated cussing, Lucky tossed out his guns. Lil knew then the first part was finished. Moments later the Texan tramped out, hands half-raised and head bowed.

'Don't try nothin', boy,' Howard warned him. 'Or yuh 'n' the bitch get it, both.'

He was thrown to the ground and tied.

'Damnit! You don't have to kick me,' he complained to his captors. 'Lil, you're a smooth talker. You had me fooled into thinkin' we'd get treated straight.'

Lil was in little position to feel sorry for him. The other possemen kept right on casting their looks at her. Some of them turned away when she glared back but the bolder ones didn't.

To get a grip on her wild thoughts, she forced herself to contemplate the outcome if she, like Lucky, was seized and prostrated. It was no hard guess what would happen. Her undress would become insanity.

'Can I go inside and grab some clothes?' she asked

urgently. The ploy of wearing none had gone past serving its purpose.

'Nope!' Howard said, leering. 'Yuh got guns in thar. Deputy Connor c'n git whatsoever's necessary fer decency. Yuh pulled one fancy stunt, an' that's more'n enough.'

The sheriff gave her no credit for defusing the situation. She'd virtually trapped Lucky, leaving him with no honourable option but to submit to arrest. Howard surely owed her a vote of thanks for that rather than orders which prolonged her exposure to the posse's disturbing inspection. Still, she and Lucky were alive and she never expected much of the corrupt 'Sheriff Coward', ever.

A little later, as they jogged back to Silver Vein, Lil and Lucky tied hand and foot to their saddles, obsequious Sly Connor congratulated Howard on his prowess.

'Sure went fine, 'xactly like you planned it, boss. Guess the wild man from Texas was just a boy full o' windy braggin', hidin' behind a female's skirts.'

Hearing him, Lil was filled with indignation.

'I don't wear skirts, Deputy, in case you've forgotten. And when your bunch sneaked up on us I was wearing nothing. Whatever Lucky was doing, it wasn't hiding. But maybe you're the only one without the imagination or enough man in him to have thought it through.'

Lucky grinned and twisted awkwardly in the saddle, his wrists lashed to the pommel.

'You're not a bit ashamed of anythin', are you, Lil?'

She looked him in the eye. 'Not one damn bit.'

*

Predictably, Howard looked for monetary profit in the arrests he'd made. The circuit judge was not scheduled to be sitting in Silver Vein for several weeks and housing prisoners in his jail created work. Howard didn't like work. He hit on the smart notion of releasing Lil to her father's care – on payment of hefty bail, of course. He also imposed the pompous, unrealistic condition that the rich cattleman 'secure help to effect her reform'.

Let others do the work! Long as he had final say, naturally, and nobody did anything that made him look smaller than them in the eyes of the community. . . .

When word of Lil's bail reached the biddies of the Silver Vein Ladies' Temperance Society, it was quickly passed to their president, Miss Purity Wadsworth. In turn, Miss Wadsworth conveyed the news to Virginia Whitpath.

'You'll remember Mr Goodnight has already attempted to procure schooling for his wayward daughter and it didn't work out,' Miss Wadsworth said.

'Yes,' Virginia said, wondering where the observation was going to lead. 'Everyone knows.'

Miss Wadsworth, who'd already thought long on the new development and was completely convinced of, and enthused by, the use to which it could be put, sighed in exasperation at what she saw as obtuseness.

'Well, don't you see? These are precisely the circumstances under which Mr Goodnight will be receptive to the suggestion that he place Lilian in the care of Dr François Guiscard!'

'Oh . . . yes,' Virginia said as the significance dawned on her. 'You mean now is a good time for Uncle and I to go calling on Mr Goodnight – to let him know about Dr Guiscard?'

'Of course,' Miss Wadsworth said, biting her lip to stop from adding 'you silly child'. Time was wasting.

'Mr Goodnight must be told before the chance is lost,' she went on. 'You must persuade Mr Goodnight quickly that a spell under the experimental treatment of Dr Guiscard would be most efficacious for his troubled young lady.'

Virginia wasn't quite sure what 'efficacious' meant but coupled with 'experimental' it had a lovely punitive ring.

Since the older woman had last spoken to her, she'd dreamed – pleasantly and several times – about Misfit Lil giving painful birth to a monstrous baby sired by a brutish French convict.

She had no idea what European criminals looked like, but the man in her dreams was like a giant mountain man with grizzled hair and beard. The beard was big and bushy; the hair hung in greasy, tightly braided strands to his shoulders. He wore a necklace of bear claws and his eyes were wild and red-rimmed, as though he was permanently drunk. Lil was scared of him and they lived in a hovel of a sod house. The oversized infant cried unceasingly.

Virginia wanted more than anything else in her small world to help mete out a real-life fate of comparably dreadful proportions to the girl she thought had stolen handsome Lucky M'Cline from her, then made her look a fool or worse by tearing off her best dress in front of the whole town and dumping her in the smithy's big water-barrel.

George Whitpath was supportive of Miss Wadsworth. He allowed that Misfit Lil remained a threat to his ward, who had suffered insult and injury at the wicked scallywag's hands.

'Ol' Ben Goodnight'll have to listen. It ain't neighbourly to refuse help.'

Accordingly, Virginia and her uncle rode their buckboard to the Flying G, helpfully armed by Miss Wadsworth with selected newspaper cuttings about the celebrated Dr Guiscard, late of Paris, France, and Taunton, Massachusetts.

Ben Goodnight, boss of the Flying G, was more than an average sort of rancher. He'd grown his outfit to enviable size on the best flats – a fine, reddish mix of sand and clay – within easy ride of Silver Vein. His corrals and grazing meadows were bounded by desolate mountains in the one direction. In the other, bleak and barren country stretched for miles like a sea of sand and rocks, the expanse broken only by sage, bunches of sandgrass and the occasional clump of piñon or juniper.

The man himself could, as the mood took him, be as forbidding as the country surrounding his domain. He had long been a widower. But he also had a quick, hearty laugh with a hint of mischief in it. He had, after all, fathered Misfit Lil and the foundation of her nature had to come from somewhere.

He was tall – a gaunt, bony man with wide shoulders and long limbs. He looked powerful and vigorous, iron-grey of hair and imperial beard and moustache. Allied with a big hawk nose and the air of a man accustomed to command, his appearance was patrician. Though he was seldom seen in town, visitors to the Flying G were met with dignity and the alert, unwinking stare of his grey eyes.

He received Virginia and George Whitpath courteously and with interest in the spacious parlour of his ranch house. This was a masculine room with no feminine knick-knacks and little in the way of ornaments on table, sideboards or mantel. But money had been spent at some time, so it had the mahogany-and-plush grandeur that would have been fitting in the house of a wealthy townsman. The ceiling was high with stained and varnished rafters. A huge stone fireplace occupied most of one wall. In front of it, a moss-green leather armchair and two upholstered chairs were arranged to make a cosy setting for conversation under a chandelier.

Goodnight motioned the Whitpaths to the chairs. The uncle wore a blue cotton shirt, bib overalls, farm boots and his best Sunday hat – a derby that seemed out of keeping with the rest. Young Miss Virginia looked about her nervously. Goodnight assessed this, wrongly as it turned out, as indicating she was a mite short of wit and possibly unstable.

But his life revolved around the business of his spread. Although he might be a good judge of what was a highly strung mare at auction, the character of human she-stuff was beyond him. He didn't recognize the deviousness in Virginia any more than he truly understood the spirit that drove his own daughter.

'You needn't be afraid,' he assured her. 'Lilian isn't allowed to mix with company. So she won't storm in and hurt you. As you know, the county's fool sheriff, Hamish Howard, has ordered I seek help to – uh – rectify her behaviour.'

George Whitpath saw his opening and stated the purpose of their visit without preliminaries.

'That's right, Mr Goodnight. It's why we came. We thought we could help.'

The cattleman's eyebrows rose. 'You did?'

'Sure. We got it all here.' He fumbled to pull out Purity Wadsworth's collection of newspaper clippings. He unfolded and tried to smooth them. 'A special doctor according to the reports. Come to Green River to give an address. An expert from Europe in the treatment of madwomen!'

'And my daughter is a madwoman?'

Whitpath flushed, realizing he'd over-stated his case. 'Well. . . .'

At this point Virginia began to prattle, rescuing her clumsy, not very articulate uncle with a parrot-like repetition of commonly held summations of Lilian's failings.

'Not to give offence, Mr Goodnight, but everyone knows your daughter has given you bother. Why, she gives it to everyone! We know that you've done all a good father could. You sent her to a fine school in Boston, and you were repaid for that by seeing her – er

– throw away the chance to be a lady. Lilian is quite unruly . . . headstrong. Like my uncle says, we only want to help. . . .'

Goodnight raised a big hand to forestall her torrent of words.

'All right, Lilian is not mad, she's headstrong. Hell, I was headstrong m'self once.'

He also wanted to say, but didn't, that he thought his girl had considerably more backbone than Virginia, whom he considered a milk-sop overly concerned with others' opinions of her, especially her uncle and aunt's.

'So hand me those bits of paper and shut up a bit while I read 'em, if that's what you've come for.'

In truth, Goodnight already knew he'd reached the end of the line in what he could do personally for Lil. He didn't want to leave her in the hands of a lazy, good-for-nothing sheriff or at the unpredictable mercy of some travelling judge.

He discovered the cuttings, describing the successes of an unorthodox medical man, a Dr François Guiscard, held out unexpected hope.

7

CATTLEMAN'S SEARCH

Ben Goodnight made infrequent visits to Silver Vein. He spruced himself up for the occasion, though no one could ever accuse him of looking the dude. In black broadcloth coat and fawn-coloured trousers, with string tie, embroidered vest and tooled boots, he cantered into town on a fine Kentucky mare.

His destination was the newspaper office. He figured to avail himself of the periodical's files of its own back numbers and of papers from as far away as Eastern seaboard cities. He was intrigued by the possibilities put to him by the Whitpaths. But he was a cautious man, and had a nagging recollection of bad reports about treatment by the French of distressed women.

The printer, who wore an eyeshade and was also the editor, chief reporter and filing clerk, waved him toward the files stacked on and under a dusty table in the darkest corner of his premises. Filing cabinets were reserved for handwritten correspondence and ledgers, though one bottom drawer held a dozen bottles of whiskey.

'Go ahead, Mr Goodnight,' the newspaper man said. 'Can I tell you anything? I've got a wide memory.'

'About this doctor feller, Guiscard. Frenchman. You know about him? Cures troubled womenfolk. I recollect something bad about how the Frenchies treat their unfortunates.

The printer scratched his balding head.

'Well, once I watched an opera put on in Salt Lake City by a foreign touring troupe. It was by a Daniel Auber who got the story from a scandalous novel by the Abbé Prevost. Was about a young woman called Manon Lescaut, met and seduced by a nobleman while she was being escorted by her brother to a convent. Manon lived in sin with the feller in Paris till she left him for a rich admirer. She was later arrested, charged with prostitution, and deported to Louisiana.'

Goodnight grunted. None of this signified much to a plain cowman like himself.

'I guess it's Guiscard himself I really need to know about.'

The printer chose and heaved several files of newspapers into a space he cleared on the table. The papers had been hole-punched in their left-hand margins and laced together with wooden slats front and back. He licked an ink-stained finger, flicked through and found news items and commentaries to recommend.

Ben Goodnight sat on a high stool pulled up by the printer, read and learned.

Dr François Guiscard was a genuine physician, it appeared, and his presence in the West was remarkable not through any lack of qualification but rather a surfeit.

In general, medicine on the frontier was roughly as practised anywhere across the continent, with extra hazards to the practitioner thrown in. More often than not, medical men had to supplement earnings. Some doubled as drugstore owners; others as preachers. They played a role in territorial and state government. Alternative business interests might be veterinary work, claim buying, mining or writing. Undertaking was seldom considered good advertisement.

Guiscard was almost pure medico, it transpired, but with foreign credentials and a strong slant toward treating sicknesses of the mind – especially woman's mind. In France, he'd been a pupil of Professor Jean-Martin Charcot, who endorsed mesmerism for the treatment of hysteria.

Guiscard had been involved in experiments examining therapeutic uses of hypnosis. Post-hypnotic suggestion had been first described at this time. Astonishing improvements in sensory acuity and memory were reported under hypnosis.

The reports Ben Goodnight read spoke mysteriously of a 'theory of dissociation'. Under hypnosis, skills and memory could be made inaccessible or recovered. Treatment was being developed for the reintegration of split personalities. Many patients suffering hysteria had been put on a path to normality.

In a dusty frontier newspaper office smelling of paper and ink, Goodnight caught a glimmering of how some of this might be made applicable to his daughter, whom folks called Misfit Lil.

Guiscard had told reporters hypnotism was a new name for the old mesmerism promulgated in the eighteenth century by the Austrian Franz Anton Mesmer.

'Some of you may have seen the mesmerized person obey the mesmerizer, accept his fictions as facts, and perform at his bidding acts of the most startling absurdity,' Dr Guiscard said. 'But when the patient recovers his senses, the spell is broken. Not so with hypnotism. The patient opens his eyes, goes away, performs the ordinary duties of life, but obeys with undeviating regularity the impulse communicated by the hypnotizer.'

Goodnight frowned and was about to ask the newspaperman a question, but noticed he had departed to the far side of his print shop. He was in deep concentration, taking pieces of 9-point type from the typecase with nimble, oily fingers and putting them into a brass typestick.

The cattleman hankered for another opinion – a living, breathing person's – but realized once he'd taken pause that he had opinions enough before him in smudgy ink on quickly browning paper from places all over. The final decision on whether he delivered up his daughter to Dr Guiscard, who had allegedly cured one of her former Boston classmates of hysteria, rested with himself alone.

Goodnight tried to imagine the situation of a patient cured of unseemly behaviour by Dr Guiscard. All the time she might believe she was acting as a free agent, but could she, in fact, have become the bond-slave of another's will?

What dangers lay in this?

Goodnight was not naive. He could imagine all sorts. But he determined to go to the telegraph office forthwith and wire Dr Guiscard while he was close by, in the territory.

Doctors were paid on a fee-for-service basis and few on the frontier, despite celebrity, were among the well-to-do. Some didn't even make a decent living. Goodnight was confident the itinerant Frenchman could be hired as easily as a cowboy riding the grub line.

He would ask the doctor if he could rectify his child's problem. He'd let him know he was financially self-sufficient after several good seasons and could find no more estimable use for his money than the correction of his Lilian's condition. But he also decided on another course he considered a wise and necessary precaution for the girl's safety.

Sadly, it turned out later to be anything but.

'I'll speak plain about this Dr Guiscard business, Miss Whitpath,' Goodnight said. It was three days gone since his call at the newspaper office and a big part of his plan was in train.

Surprised at his visit to her uncle's humble ranch house, Virginia said, 'Of course, Mr Goodnight. Please do. We held no brief for Dr Guiscard, but wanted to do a neighbourly thing.' She shuddered delicately. 'I've reason to know how hurtful your daughter can be, and the notion of a girl being in continuing conflict with her father . . . it's awful. Disrespectful.'

'That I can abide, but the county is looking to me for a solution.'

'Of course, it's why we presented the newspaper cuttings.'

Goodnight nodded gravely. 'But I've been and looked. Not all the eastern Johnnies write so highly of Dr Guiscard. He could be a charlatan. Listen, young woman, I've rented the old Whittaker house in town for a special refuge – where my gal can be boarded and treated privately by the doc. Yet my investment might be wasted. And it also came to me that if the doc's a sham, he could be a rogue of any other stripe to boot.'

'Oh. . . . .'

Virginia was puzzled and felt a stirring of disappointment. Was the hope Mr Goodnight had held out, that Misfit Lil was due to receive a comeuppance at the hands of a harsh French doctor, about to be dashed?

'I need to avoid the consequences if I've made a mistake in judgement,' Goodnight went on, 'and moreover, the wagging of the town's malicious tongues. Dr Guiscard will need a nurse, and Lilian, a chaperon. If your aunt and uncle can spare you, I thought the position might suit yourself. You're of an age with my gal and could provide companionship as she takes the cure.'

Virginia blinked in surprise. She realized all was not lost after all. In fact, it was turning out better than ever. She was being offered a box-seat from where she could witness what she'd been given every cause to believe would be the taming and breaking of Misfit Lil! Miss Purity Wadsworth would envy her.

'Why, that sounds a perfectly wonderful idea, Mr Goodnight,' she said warmly. 'And I'm sure my folks will oblige. Thank you very much for thinking of me. The position will be an honour.'

Sternly, Goodnight said, 'Mind, I don't want to hear back one report of impropriety in the arrangements for my daughter. Everything must be done honestly and above board, with yourself in attendance, helping the doctor.'

'You can rest assured of that, Mr Goodnight. I understand perfectly what has to be done.'

While Virginia Whitpath was delighted with Ben Goodnight's provisions, his daughter was disgusted.

'Pa, you're a godawful fool!' Lil said bluntly. 'I ain't scared of any Frenchie doc and don't need soppy Virginia Whitpath to hold my hand. She'd be the last person in the world a girl would look to for defence if'n a man should have mischief on his mind. Where did you get such a notion?'

Ben Goodnight sighed wearily.

'Virginia Whitpath isn't the sort to let anybody do what she doesn't want them to do.'

'Yeah, but how do we know what she wouldn't want them to do? She purely hates me for settling her hash outside the smithy.'

'To tell the truth, gal, I thought you'd prefer someone on hand you knew you could handle. Fact is, you're deep in trouble with the law. Siding with Lucky M'Cline put you in it and left me in a poor position. M'Cline's fight wasn't your'n and this could be your let-off.'

After a moment's glowering silence, Lil accepted in her mind that angry defiance was going to lead nowhere.

'All right. I go along with the crazy charade of seeing this snake-oil merchant, or whatever he is. Then I go free, is that it?'

'It's possible. Howard's got the law backing him. But he wants nothing 'cept easy dinero and I've paid plenty in so-called bail. Howsomever, the undertaking to get your ways mended has to be seen as being fulfilled.'

Lil groaned beneath her breath and gritted out an oath.

'God! It sounds like things have gotten a mite desperate around here. I wish Jackson was about. He'd know what to do.'

'Forget Mr Farraday, gal. He's away guiding in the Henry Mountains.'

'Yep, no counting on help there. Meanwhile, I figure you're going to get fleeced by some fancy doctor whose name sure don't register with me! Why would he've come trekking West if he was so all-fired famous?'

Her father coloured a little under her candid criticism.

'Carry on ranting thisaway,' he said huffily, 'and I'll begin to think you are suffering from hysteria.'

Lil finally relented and agreed to co-operate. After all, she'd done many a more daring deed than accept treatment from a doctor. Like her father, she figured she'd be safe enough. Guiscard would have to be very stupid to do anything that wasn't on the level with another girl of the district in attendance.

How could he ever get to be sure Virginia wouldn't tell on him, ruining his reputation and his professional life? Why, she might even blackmail him for all he knew!

No, going along with the tomfoolery was safe enough.

8

FIRST DUEL

Lil stationed herself at the bay window of the room allocated to her in the rented Whittaker house. She knew the big property of old and had chosen the room herself because the jutting window gave her a clear view of one side of Silver Vein's Main Street and fair glimpses of most of the other.

She was watching for the return of Virginia Whitpath from a trip to the town's shops. The girl – in her new freedom from the discipline of her aunt and uncle – did love to haunt the mercantile and the haberdashery, buying all manner of feminine fripperies! Lil had no time for such trivia, of course.

She had a vague sense of unease, mingled with anticipation. It was the third day after the arrival of Dr François Guiscard in Silver Vein and the beginning of her stay in the new place of custody. The doctor had promised that today her treatment sessions would begin in earnest. But, of course, they couldn't start without his assistant and her chaperon, namely, Virginia.

Guiscard had arrived on a regular run of the stagecoach from Green River and been met by her father, herself and Virginia Whitpath. It had been her last, brief taste of limited freedom. Her lot these days seemed to be bound by four walls – a sheriff's office cell, a room at the Flying G, the old Whittaker residence. It was scarcely better than death for a spirit more at home in the wide outdoors of range, mountain and canyonlands.

Dr Guiscard had stepped down, trippingly, awkwardly, from the coach; a queer, spare-boned, stoop-shouldered buzzard in a black clawhammer coat. A day's stubble and the grime of travel had been on his face, which he'd since shaved clean. Lil and her father had run their eyes over him with the frank curiosity of true Westerners toward a stranger.

He had a mane of silver hair and a long, pale, hatchet-like face with a high forehead and a lantern jaw. You were impressed that he was no weak man when you looked into his deep-set eyes. All his power seemed to be concentrated in the eyes – dark but glowing with a fervour that was almost fanaticism.

By some misunderstanding, he'd hit upon the notion that Virginia was the patient he'd been summoned to attend. When it was made clear she wasn't, he'd showed what had seemed pleasure.

He'd looked Lil up and down, calculatingly, and said in a high-pitched voice only slightly cracked by foreign accent, 'Ah, good! The fair girl is *très belle* but this one will respond better. The doctors at the most famous women's infirmary in Paris assure us it is the case – *toujours* a result can be accomplished *plus rapidement* with dark girls – and my experience at your American state insane asylum in Taunton, Massachusetts, agrees with them.'

Lil hadn't liked being referred to as a case, or the implication that she was a lunatic, but she'd thought it too soon to make clear that any similar disrespect he showed – or resultant liberties he took – would be resented.

Now a crucial time was approaching along with Virginia, who came into sight hurrying back to the house, basket over arm, to attend to her duties as a nurse.

Lil found some amusement in the situation. For little events and exchanges she'd already observed hinted to a sharp and knowing person like herself that the other girl might be in greater danger than herself from whatever predatory inclinations she suspected the strange doctor harboured.

Instinct told her Guiscard was crooked. Whether his crime was in conning desperate folks like her father, or in something deeper, she didn't yet know.

But unlike herself, the purely raised Virginia saw no reason to be on her guard.

Dr Guiscard had taken the front parlour of the house, uncovered and rearranged the dust-draped furniture and declared it to be his study and office. Lil took no exception to this. The two-storey frame house had been built by Flash Sam Whittaker, who'd run a now-defunct gambling hall in whose collapse she and Jackson Farraday had played a stirring part. One of the finest residences in Silver Vein, it had been vacant, off and on, since Flash Sam's shooting death in Green River. Too pretentious for Lil's taste, most rooms being papered and carpeted, she cared little who claimed its best accommodations, and for what purpose, although her father was paying the rent.

Lil was summoned to the so-called office shortly after Virginia returned from her shopping expedition. With high but differing degrees of expectation, the girls made their way down the stairway, dignified by the slim curve of its mahogany balustrade, through the panelled hallway, and entered the big room where Dr Guiscard awaited them.

The room was very quiet with the quietness bestowed by the muffling of heavy, luxurious drapes, which were drawn, and the thick carpet. Dr Guiscard, tall and silver-haired, rose from behind a desk on which stood a lighted lamp.

'Come in, ladies, come in. The time has come to deliver you from your demons, Miss Lilian.'

'What are you going to do to her?' Virginia asked, unable to contain her curiosity.

He laughed, with a false note. 'Nothing bad – if she's good! Will you please loosen your clothing and sit, Miss Lilian. Right here in this comfortable armchair. So!'

He pulled up a chair for himself, facing the armchair and adjusted the position of the lamp so they would be within the bright pool of its light.

Lilian shrugged. 'Well, all right. I've never messed with the likes of this mesmerism poppycock before. And I'm not sure I'll want to do it again once the obligation is over. But it's going to be damned interesting knowing you, watching you operate. It sure will.'

Virginia licked her upper lip and swallowed as though her mouth was watering.

'How brave you are, Lil!'

Lil chose not to see it that way.

'Given the choice of a term in some kind of reformatory or humouring the doc, my pa and Hamish Howard, I'll take the humouring. Can't do real harm. Sooner it's done, the less Flying G money goes into Guiscard's pockets, as I figure it.'

Guiscard raised his eyebrows. 'Do I detect scepticism in your voice, Miss Goodnight?'

Lil gave him a long, steady look.

'I've seen more'n a few games that've proved too hot for their players to handle, and I guess yours will be just another.'

The doctor heaved a sigh and placed his hands together, fingertip to fingertip.

'You must get used to the idea that we will not be playing a game, young lady. The scientific study of *Le Magnétisme Animal* of Dr Franz Mesmer was commenced forty years ago by Dr James Braid, a Manchester surgeon, who gave it the new name hypnosis. You may sneer all you like if you desire to display the Western, rural ignorance. Today, hypnotic behavioural modification is the big news in Europe and the Eastern cities. Demonstrations are common.'

'Oh, demonstrations,' Lil flashed back. 'Do tell.'

'*Certainement.* Doubters volunteer their services as subjects – to ridicule the practitioners by exposing them as fakes. They say they cannot be hypnotized against their will and would not do things they would not normally do. But despite initial resistance, they are brought under the hypnotist's control and thus confounded.'

'Hmm!' Lil reacted witheringly. 'How long is this going to take? Living in a fine town house ain't in my line of riding at all. When do you hand over my bill of health?'

'Don't play the fool. Depending on a patient's state of mind, the treatment could take days or weeks.'

Unable to disguise her avid interest, Virginia cut in with a question. 'What's the difference between mesmerism and hypnotism?'

Lil noted Guiscard was not loath to display his knowledge.

'*Mais oui,* Miss Whitpath – you show admirable intelligence in your question! Hypnotism is not a new thing, its differences being extensions of the old mesmerism. Yet suggestions put to a hypnotized subject are acted upon when the hypnotic state has to all appearances passed away, and not during the trance as in mesmerism. Everyone has seen the person from the theatre audience obey the stage mesmerist – accept his fiction as fact and perform at his bidding acts that are amusingly risqué. But when the patient recovers his or her senses, the spell is broken. That is not the case with hypnotism. The patient awakens, walks about, goes away, performs the ordinary duties of life – but obeys impulses communicated by the hypnotizer.'

'See, Virginia?' Lil said. 'It's a travesty – a theatre stunt, like a burlesque-and-leg show. Competition for *The Black Crook* or Miss Lydia Thompson and her British Blondes!'

Miss Thompson's notorious performances had begun in New York in 1868 but her troupe had embarked on a series of nationwide tours that had continued ten years and reached as far west as Virginia City, Nevada. Lil's ridicule was scathing, since the public, which loved the leg-art shows, nevertheless recognized them for what a strait-laced critic had condemned as a 'bewilderment of limbs, belladonna and greasepaint'; an import of no serious import.

Guiscard drew himself up, offended.

'This is not vaudeville, Miss Goodnight. Perhaps you would like a small and visible demonstration of my powers. Miss Whitpath can be our witness and the adjudicator. Are you agreeable?'

Lil could never resist a challenge.

'Sure. Let me take a first dose of my medicine, and you'll see how it gets spat up! What do I have to do?'

'It is not very easy. The criteria are you must first clear your mind of opposition, and you must be at ease, without the rigidity in your muscles, and comfortable. And it is best that the subject believes she can be hypnotized. Which will be a tall order for this smart Misfit Lil!'

Goaded, Lil said, 'I can try. . . . Anything to get us through this nonsense pronto. Watch the doctor closely if I go into a trance, Virginia. No ungentlemanly conduct – understand what I mean?'

Lil confidently expected that Dr Guiscard would be unable to hypnotize her, but he produced a silver locket on a chain, which he dangled in the light of the lamp, ordering Lil to fix her gaze on it intently.

'Don't take your eyes off it for a moment, or the experiment cannot begin.'

Lil co-operated willingly, sure that the trial would expose the Frenchman as a fake. But she soon began to feel fatigued. Who could have thought watching a gently swinging object could do that?

Not that she'd admit it, of course. Beyond the locket, which shone brightly in the lamplight, were two other glowing orbs. Well, if Guiscard could stare at the locket and not look away, so could she!

Guiscard talked in a low tone, lulling her into relaxation.

'Do you feel sleepy, Miss Goodnight?'

'Yeah. . . .' she managed, but then her vocal cords seemed to lapse into a paralysis, along with everything else. Moreover, she must have indeed fallen asleep and for how long she didn't know.

When she became aware of her surroundings again, the drapes at the windows had been pulled back, letting in the daylight and she was alone with Virginia Whitpath. It was as though she'd come out of a momentary day-dream. She blinked her eyes against the light.

'God . . . what happened? Where's the doc?'

'Oh, you've come back!' Virginia said. 'It was so interesting. I wouldn't have missed it for worlds. Dr Guiscard needed to visit the bank, but he said we were to return to your room and I was to note carefully everything that happens – that you would receive proof of his powers. Isn't it fascinating?'

Lil shook her head sadly at the girl's gullibility.

'No, Virginia, it's mumbo-jumbo though I do admit the quack sent me to sleep concentrating on his boring locket.'

'But he put you into a trance. I saw it!'

'Tchah! He just made it look like he did. Did I do anything except doze?'

'Why, no. . . .' Virginia faltered. 'Your eyes dilated and then they closed.'

'So there you are. I fell asleep is all.'

But Virginia persisted, frustrated, Lil thought, that her petty revenge so far had not been exacted for her.

'What I am allowed to tell you,' the untrusted companion said, 'without spoiling the doctor's unveiling of his bona fides, is that the James Braid he mentioned is the Father of Modern Hypnotism. Dr Braid rejected Mesmer's idea that hypnosis was induced by magnetism. He proved that the mesmeric trance is a physio – a physio-something process. Anyhow, it results from prolonged attention to a bright moving object – like the locket Dr Guiscard employed. Lengthy fixation with the eyes fatigues certain parts of the brain and causes a trance – a nervous sleep or, from the Greek, neuro-hypnosis.'

'My, quite the little expert he's made you, hasn't he?' Lil said.

Virginia ignored her sarcasm and became mysterious when she tried to question her further.

Lil said, 'Huh, no nevermind, Miss High-and-Mighty Whitpath. I'm still in one piece, ain't I? And he hasn't changed me a bit, has he?'

'He didn't try to. He told me – this time he only entered your unconscious mind sufficiently to plant the proofs that hypnotism isn't the nonsense you claim. The resolution of your problems will take longer, but it will come.'

Lil scoffed. 'You really believe that?'

Gleefully, Virginia replied, 'Eventually Dr Guiscard will be able to work on your deep, entrenched personal problems, Lil Goodnight! He'll break down your rough and unladylike patterns of behaviour.'

Lil laughed openly.

'I don't think so!'

'Just wait, Lil . . . just wait one or two more hours. We'll have a sign of the doctor's abilities this very afternoon. He promised.'

9

THE MESMERIST'S BRAND

The girls waited in Lil's room, observing the passing traffic into town and dipping into the pages of old, orange-covered dime novels left by a former tenant. The stories were melodramatic, short on wilderness fact as it was known to Lil and long on predictable perils and romantic rescues.

Virginia, who believed in their excesses, found them scandalous. Lil was only mildly amused by their exaggerations and inaccuracies.

To Lil's sharp but assuredly untrained eye, nothing had happened to her during her so-called trance. She knew she was physically intact and untouched.

But Virginia kept smiling to herself, as though victory was hers.

When Lil again probingly broached the subject of what Guiscard had done while she dozed, Virginia said smugly, 'Nothing and everything. You can't always be right, Lil.'

Time passed. Dr Guiscard appeared on the street outside the Ranchers' and Miners' Bank with the new young teller, Ossie Caldeen, and the pair went into the restaurant at Ma Coutts's Traveller's Hotel.

Eventually, Guiscard returned alone to his office in the house and they heard the lock click noisily as he turned the key, which told them he wasn't to be disturbed.

Mid-afternoon, when outside the sun was beginning to sink into the blue western sky and its rays shone directly into their eyrie, a strained expression came into Lil's face.

'Ow!' she cried. 'My arm – it's burning!'

Virginia dropped her book, face flushed with excitement.

'Let's see it, Lil! Do let's see!'

Lil pulled up her sleeve.

'Oh, my God!' she said.

They both examined Lil's left forearm, eyes wide and staring at what they were seeing.

'Yes!' Virginia breathed triumphantly. 'The promise is fulfilled.'

What looked like a burn or brand had appeared on the previously tanned but unblemished skin, roughly drawn in the shape of a letter G as though with a running iron. At several of the turns, where the mark was deeper, beads of blood appeared.

'The bastard!' Lil cried. 'He must've put an iron on me!'

Virginia looked like a cat sampling what she expected would be the first of many bowls of cream.

'But you know he didn't. You wouldn't take my word, and I watched you take off your coat and pants to check all over for evidence of interference. You did that in this very room not two hours since . . . *after* Dr Guiscard had gone out.'

'What happened then?' Lil asked flatly, trying not to grimace at the soreness of her arm.

Virginia enjoyed explaining.

'Dr Guiscard said that Professor Charcot and his pupils at the Salpêtrière in Paris often produced the effect of burns on the skin of hypnotized subjects by means of suggestion. The idea of the burn does not take effect immediately, but after the lapse of some hours. All the doctor did was lightly trace the G on your arm with his index finger.'

Virginia said that Guiscard had also spoken in a stern monotone, implanting a powerful suggestion in her mind: 'This afternoon at four o'clock, the lines I trace will appear in relief on your skin, bright red as a burn.'

'Isn't that wonderful?' Virginia finished.

'Goddamnit! No,' Lil said. 'I don't understand how this trick was pulled, but now it'll be harder than ever to stop the asshole from messing with my mind.'

Could he really change her nature? Could he by hypnotic techniques change her – over many sessions spread across days and weeks – into the 'acceptable' person she wasn't and didn't want to be?

Lil was out of her depth and knew it. The only person she had to turn to was the simpering Virginia, whose main aim in the business was surely to exact a petty revenge for Lil's supposed seduction of her beau, Lucky M'Cline.

Meanwhile, her father was probably going to be robbed blind by the crooked Dr Guiscard.

She groaned in exasperation. If only her friend, the army's civilian scout Jackson Farraday, mature and wise in the ways of the world in life, was on hand to lend advice. . . . He would know what to do; maybe would have already done it.

But he wasn't around. He was still miles away in the Henry Mountains, guiding a scientific expedition.

In the study of the rented house, Dr François Guiscard quietly sipped brandy from a large glass and congratulated himself. His villainy and mental powers, not to mention his aspirations to wealth, were greater than either of the house's girl tenants suspected. And he had plans for both of them.

The main scheme was simple in its basics, if not its detail, as all great campaigns are.

Timing would be everything, but Guiscard had faith he could arrange matters quickly. The dark girl, Lil, was feisty, but her nature – her free and open ways – also made her receptive to suggestion, as he'd already proved. He'd made the first steps to fatigue the nerve-ends of her sense organs. Frequent repetition of this temporary, paralysing fatigue would predispose his patient to fall ever more readily into a state of trance.

Once she was in this state, he'd act to place the neutral, unsuspecting aide, Virginia, into similar catalepsy, so she would recall and report nothing. Then, by furthering Lil's fatigue, her paralysis could be moved progressively inwards to the sense-centres in the brain itself and a control established. While Lil's ego was absent, and the brain rendered passive, it would be easy for him to implant ideas of certain actions in it, these ideas to be carried out later when a new trance was induced by the voicing of trigger words and the presentation of prompting symbols.

Lil's actions would be witnessed by the ignorant western townsfolk as though they were entirely Lil's own – though she would be merely the agent of her hypnotizer, himself. No suspicion or blame would be attached to Dr Guiscard when his patient 'escaped' from his care.

He chuckled quietly to himself at the fortuitous way the opportunity had been put before him, at his cleverness in taking advantage, and at how he would outmanoeuvre the scornful Miss Goodnight.

The rich cattleman's daughter had a staggering reputation as a 'bad lot' and nobody would be the least bit surprised when she held up the Silver Vein Ranchers' and Miners' Bank, to rob it of a big mining company's monthly payroll, which was due to be delivered within the week and securely locked up in the huge safe in the manager's office. Because everyone in this country feared their quaintly dubbed Princess of Pistoleers' prowess with her Colts, none would dare refuse the demands she'd make.

Lil would cache the loot someplace he could collect it himself later, after seeing that she was delivered to

Sheriff Hamish Howard for an appropriate return to his jail and to shoulder all the blame. Unaware of the crime she'd committed, the hapless girl would volubly, futilely deny it.

What a joke that would be! Guiscard swirled his brandy and inhaled its rich aroma. He chuckled again, a little louder.

Ossie Caldeen, the teller he'd recruited as his accomplice inside the bank, would not be paid the share of the payroll money he'd been promised. An unfortunate accident would be arranged. With the loss of his patient, Guiscard would then regrettably pull stakes and quietly quit Silver Vein with Lilian Goodnight's bank haul, leaving no one to tell tales.

One last refinement of his plan concerned the other girl, the fair and pretty simpleton, Virginia Whitpath. A sweet creature even if the one called Misfit Lil was not! He would look forward to rewarding himself for his smartness by making a woman of her. A little extra pleasure after business was done. . . .

He'd been obliged by circumstances to abstain for many weeks and he was in good condition for it. His appetite had not been satisfied, only whetted, by studying a slim volume called *La Science Pratique*, which had forty pretty little plates. In full possession of her senses, the young American beauty wouldn't show off her treasure as enticingly, of course, but put under his influence she could be counted upon to accommodate him.

Outside the window, an eagle wheeled slowly above the town on spread wings.

'I will be a monarch, like that big bird, soaring above the common silly hicks,' Dr Guiscard murmured. 'Whatever Lilian Goodnight and Virginia Whitpath might protest after the matter is completed, will be unsubstantiated allegation. No one will be able to touch me.'

The crime took place over five minutes on what had hitherto been a quiet and lazy summer's morning in the small Utah township. Afterwards, Misfit Lil was adamant she hadn't been there and hadn't done it.

No one believed her. Her own despairing father didn't believe her. But the cold facts of all other reports said Lil robbed the Silver Vein bank at gunpoint.

The few citizens ambling peacefully about their business or lounging on the plankwalk outside McHendry's saloon, waiting for it to open, paid little attention when Lilian Goodnight collected her grey cow pony from the livery stable and hitched him to the rail outside the Ranchers' and Miners' Bank.

Nor did they see much amiss when she pulled up a red bandanna over her face and threw two stout, hide saddle-bags, roped together, over her shoulder. In her men's duds, she was a strange girl who did strange things, and everyone knew she had lately been under the care of a foreign doctor whose specialty was treating delusion in females.

Lil strode into the bank in her familiar, long-legged way and was forgotten.

Only one customer was present in the banking chamber, the Reverend Titus Fisher. Lil whipped out a

Colt revolver, the well-worn wooden handle settling in a strong hand like it naturally belonged there, and told him in even, determined tones, 'Don't you holler. Reverend, I'm to rob the bank. Get down on the floor and put your hands at the back of your head.'

Fisher blinked as though he couldn't believe his eyes, but he did as he was told with alacrity, going down on his knees, with which he was familiar, then prostrating himself on the floor. Whatever folks thought about Lil's strangeness, they knew she knew her business when it came to guns. Fisher had visions of disablement or death but none of an imminent hereafter.

He didn't think to pray; to ask for divine intervention or guidance. All he twittered was, 'Well I never! Well I never!'

Lil turned her attention to teller Ossie Caldeen behind his grille. She was waving her gun.

Though apprehensive, Caldeen spoke lines which no one except himself knew he'd been given to say. He was careful to be word-perfect and he also produced a silver locket he'd been given. In truth, the thin, pale-faced young man had as little faith in this talisman as the Reverend Fisher had in his Bible teaching, but it did seem to draw Lil Goodnight's peculiarly glazed stare.

'The manager's office is the door on your left. You know what to do.' Then, like the frightened preacher but without being ordered, Caldeen got down on his knees, lay flat and trusted to luck.

The scene continued to be played out in the office of the burly, middle-aged manager, Leo Brennan. Questioned later, Brennan testified as follows:

'You're quite certain it was Misfit Lil?'

'Positive. Kicked open the door and swaggered in big as life. With face masked or not, I'd not mistake the boyish but female figure anyplace. I was startled.'

'What did she say?'

'I'd just been to the safe and had my back to her, locking it up. She said something like I could unlock it again, fast.'

'And you did?'

'Sure. She spoke real plain and I was menaced with a gun. Everybody knows she can shoot the pip out of an ace at twenty yards, so I opened up quick. I figured my life was worth more than the money.'

'How much money was it, Leo?'

'Twenty thousand in greenbacks and mint gold and silver. I put it in the saddle-bags she threw on the floor beside me. I told her she wouldn't get away with it.'

'Did she dispute that?'

'Nope. She only told me to shut up. She didn't seem somehow to be thinking about anything, if you know what I mean. I guess these desperadoes who take to the outlaw trail just don't.'

'Folks say they heard some shots.'

'When the safe was cleaned out, she told me to raise my hands and get behind my desk . . . said it was all mighty serious and I was to be careful. But when she moved to the door with the two bulging bags, she turned to take the key out of the lock. I dived for a pistol I keep in the top desk drawer, ducked down and shot. My aim was naturally more than a mite wild and the bullet went into the wall.'

'She fired back?'

'Sure she did. Took a chunk off the edge of the desk. I got even lower and she left, slamming the door after her and turning the key outside.'

In the banking chamber, Caldeen and Fisher were still on the floor, trembling. Lil tore out of the bank, leaped into her saddle and sent the grey into a quick gallop out of town.

She was well away before the good folk of Silver Vein realized that their bank had been robbed.

10

'MAD-BITCH KILLER!'

In a tone that defied contradiction Sheriff Hamish Howard told Deputy Sly Connor that their bailiwick had seen the last of Misfit Lil.

Given his character (or lack of it), it was no surprise that he didn't admit his mistake when Lil rode back into town late the same day, stabled her horse at the livery and returned to the rented ex-Whittaker residence and the care of Dr François Guiscard.

In Howard's defence, it had to be stated that another startling development in the meantime could have caused him to forget his bold pronouncement.

Ossie Caldeen had taken his normal midday meal break and afterward declared a strong desire to take a stroll in the open air to calm his nerves. He remained 'all shook up' by the hold-up. Leo Brennan had excused him and shut up the bank. The manager said he felt sick to the stomach himself every time he thought of the stolen twenty thousand.

Caldeen had made tracks for a clump of woodland, north of the township and off the stage road that eventually passed through Green River. It was here that his body was found by a small boy exercising his dog after school was out. The shocked button ran back to town and home to his mother pell-mell.

Reluctantly, because he had enough unavoidable work on his plate taking statements about the bank robbery, Hamish Howard went to the scene to check out the story. A dead man was all it would take to ruin totally what was left of his disrupted day. But the indignant mother had made it plain that the chore was nothing less than a sheriff's duty. He couldn't afford not to investigate if he expected to keep, come next election, what most all of the time was a cosy sinecure.

Down under the tangle of willow and scrub, there was indeed a very lifeless body: Ossie Caldeen's. The bank teller had been shot through the head at close range. A neat, third eye had been placed in his pallid brow. Seen from the other side, the exit wound at the back of his head was an ugly, bloody mess. The collar and back of his suit coat were wet and black, greasy with jellied blood. A swarm of flies rose, buzzing angrily, when the body was turned.

Puffing and blowing, Howard jumped to the conclusion that Caldeen's murder was connected with the bank robbery, not simply because he wasn't stupid – as he was passing fond of assuring the local citizenry

– but because it conveniently removed the need for further inquiries. The man had been shot because he'd been a witness to a crime. The perpetrator of that crime was Misfit Lil. No question about it. Therefore she also had to be Caldeen's killer. Case solved.

When Lil came back to her lodging, where she'd been under the supervision of Dr Guiscard, Howard rejoiced. A swift arrest was made with the doctor's fullest co-operation and the expression of his profuse regrets at her 'unsanctioned outing'.

Lil was returned to the Silver Vein jail, again locked in a cell alongside Lucky M'Cline, her erstwhile partner in hell-raising. She declared over and over that she knew nothing of any bank robbery.

Howard was flabbergasted at the temerity of her denials.

'Witnesses swear yuh did it. Yuh callin' Leo Brennan and the Reverend Fisher – a man o' the cloth – liars?'

Lil was uncommonly flustered. 'Yes – no!'

'Now git your story straight, gal – which is it?'

'Well, maybe I did rob the bank. Dr Guiscard has been treating me under hypnotism. He must've made me do it, instead of mending my bad habits, as he was supposed to.'

Howard laughed hollowly. 'Huh! Seems to me them habits've gotten worse! How'd yuh account fer that? An' what did yuh do with the payroll money?'

Lil couldn't answer. 'You'll have to ask the doc.'

'Now see here. I don't swaller this mesmerism stuff. Yuh're usin' it as a new means to git your sluttish, wicked way an' dodge the consequences. It's jest moonshine fer the soft-brains. Sheer bluff!'

'But it's not! I can show you evidence.' Eagerly, Lil rolled up her left sleeve. 'See here – Dr Guiscard put a brand on my arm. He did it by planting a suggestion in my mind while I was mesmerized. It's a letter G. For Guiscard, arranged as proof to me of his power.'

Howard thought about it for a moment, scowling. Would Lil Goodnight be able to convince a judge with this pattern of broken blisters, still red and new?

Hell, no, he could soon shoot this down!

'Haw . . . I don't reckon so. It's G fer Goodnight. An' yuh put it there your ownself. It's a trick t' blacken the doc; a smokescreen t' throw dust in the law's eyes.'

Lil was frustrated and furious. Howard *was* stupid, although he thought he wasn't.

'You can't have it both ways. If the brand's G for Goodnight, how can it also be a trick to shift suspicion to Guiscard?'

Howard was growing red in the face.

'Yuh're honest-t'-God crazy, Lil Goodnight,' he blustered. 'Yuh shot Ossie Caldeen. Yuh turned mad-bitch killer! No one's gonna listen t' your smart mouth no more!'

Damn; Lil had a chilling fear he was right.

'Sheriff, stop being obstinate about this,' she pleaded. 'You have to question Guiscard! Ask him where he was when Ossie Caldeen was killed. I *know* I wouldn't have done that. Why should I?'

' 'Cause he were an eye-witness when yuh stuck up the bank,' Howard said.

'No! He was killed by Guiscard so he couldn't be

made to talk or need to be paid off.' Lil was remembering something as she spoke. 'He was Guiscard's accomplice. I saw them together, going into Ma Coutts's restaurant.'

Howard jeered. 'More fairy-tales! Lots o' folks go inta the restaurant. . . . Or maybe Caldeen was your accomplice, an' it was you who had to wipe him out.'

Lil clenched her fists, and raised and shook them over her head.

'Goddamnit!' she cried to the heavens. 'You don't want to understand!'

'Shuddup, slut! It ain't a question o' my understandin'.' Howard turned his back on Lil and walked away from the bars between them.

He'd made it brutally obvious to her he didn't care for digging out any truth that would support her seemingly implausible explanations. Rights and wrongs didn't matter if they looked like they might not suit his political agenda.

Pinning terrible crimes on Lil would please a raft of voters. Miss Purity Wadsworth and the members of her Ladies' Temperance Society would be delighted to see an end to her career in irreverence. Female suffrage was the norm in Utah and – battleaxes to a woman – the married temperance women would also ensure their husbands cast their ballots in Howard's favour next election. Likewise, the congregation of Titus Fisher would also be happy to vote for the man who'd fixed the embarrassing Misfit Lil.

Had she ever been in a tighter corner?

*

Guiscard's former patient had been jailed two days, awaiting the coming of the circuit judge and what promised to be a show trial, when the doctor announced almost casually that he was pulling stakes in the territory. Other places were calling for his talents and he no longer had reason to stay. Lilian Goodnight had been delivered into the hands of justice and he'd made a detailed, sworn statement on the case, which was lodged with Sheriff Hamish Howard.

He'd also confessed to anyone who cared to listen, including her despairing father, that Lilian Goodnight had been an impossible case – a delinquent and hysteric quite beyond the reach of even the finest minds of Paris's Salpêtrière. Nothing remained for him to do in Silver Vein. . . .

That, of course, was not the truth. Most importantly, he had to pick up two stout, hide saddle-bags. If Lil had completed her instructions satisfactorily – and she doubtless had – these were carefully wrapped in a waterproof tarp and hidden under rocks close to the old mining-engineer's shack where she'd lived as a squatter. But he was telling no one that.

And he had another, smaller but still delectable secret: his control over the mind of Virginia Whitpath had been perfected, virtually without her knowledge.

In the kitchen of the Whittaker house, Guiscard prepared a potion of chocolate with his own hand. He laced the beverage with certain drugs guaranteed to raise amorous propensities. Not that the drugs would be required, of course, but they might be a beneficial ancillary.

Frequent repetition of certain exercises he'd set Virginia 'for the improvement of her mind' had predisposed the co-operative she-noodle to fall readily into a state of trance. As a test, he'd read her a poem while she was hypnotized and she'd repeated it back to him perfectly. Awake, she'd forgotten it completely. On being re-hypnotized, she'd repeated it again.

He knew now that, under hypnosis, she would act upon anything he suggested to her without demur. A little physical force might be required, of course, but no actual violence, and he would rise to the occasion nobly. After the event, the dear nymph would have no memory of the initiation she'd consented to.

But arrogant villain that Guiscard was, he erred in taking all he fancied as though it were his God-given right. An oversight as he fantasized about the pleasure about to be his led him to overplay his hand.

When Virginia Whitpath awoke she found what little of her clothing she was wearing had been tossed up to her waist. How this had come about, she had no recollection.

She did remember talking with Dr Guiscard. They'd been discussing his imminent departure from Silver Vein. The plans were that the house would be closed up and that she would return to her aunt and uncle's ranchhouse with a suitable bonus for her services in the care of Misfit Lil, who'd undone herself beyond Virginia's most vengeful dreams.

And they'd been drinking chocolate.

Beyond that, she had only two brief, phantom

memories divided by a spell of oblivion. Both were like dreams. The first memory was of an overwhelming, breathtakingly sharp pain. The second was of her own voice crying out.

Had she been drugged? Mesmerized?

Panic! As her senses returned, Virginia discovered she was not lying in her own room, but on the four-poster bed in the house's grandest bedroom, which had hitherto been set aside solely for the privacy of Dr Guiscard.

The late, high-living Flash Sam Whittaker's tastes in luxurious accommodation had inspired him to furnish his spacious, personal bedchamber with an elaborate washstand on which stood fine porcelain that looked to be of Dresden manufacture. Plump velvet cushions, richly coloured with royal blue or red predominant, sat on various chairs. Others were scattered on the floor. But most notably, considerable expense had been gone to in the provision of glass. Two walls and the ceiling were inlaid with large plate mirrors. Wherever Virginia looked, she saw her own reflection.

Perhaps this had not bothered the clever, self-assured French doctor, but to Virginia it was disconcerting. No, she corrected herself, it was more: it was horribly frightening, given that all the mirrored self-images threw her state of undress at her as a kind of brazen taunt. This couldn't be her! Not Miss Virginia Whitpath of irreproachable reputation.

Seeing her predicament multiplied and magnified in an encirclement of looking-glasses was as unsettling an experience as being ducked in the smith's water-barrel in her underthings. Worse!

Quickly, she shook off her lethargy, and curled her body protectively so that less was revealed. She felt no better; colder, if anything, and with a sudden, compelling urge to go use the large *pot de chambre* she could glimpse in the bottom of a mahogany wardrobe, the doors of which had been left ajar.

She was also becoming aware of a cramping feeling in her stomach and a terrible soreness of a kind she'd never experienced before.

Thoroughly alarmed, she rolled off the bed, setting each of the mirror Virginias in sickening motion. She walked across the room. Somehow she was expecting to waddle like a duck, or to amble bow-legged like a man who'd been too long on horseback. But she did neither. She just felt stretched, as though something was still inside her.

As she sat, tears began to roll down her face. There was no describing her burning pain. Nor, once she was done, did the throbbing ache and the soreness go away.

Part of myself has been given up, she thought. The feeling was way beyond any strangeness she'd imagined whenever she'd wondered how it might be.

She also saw, from her new low angle, that her discarded clothing was folded and draped over the back of an upholstered, gilt-wood chair covered back and seat in a showy, floral fabric. The garments had been folded and draped correctly and conscientiously – exactly in the neat manner she would have done it herself, so that nothing was creased or spoiled.

It was then, standing up, that she noticed the

damning spots of blood on the crumpled white sheets of the big bed that still bore the impression of bodies.

The humiliation and sense of degradation were too much. She could restrain herself no longer and began to cry in earnest over her loss.

Virginia did indeed have no memory of recent events, but Dr Guiscard had been very rash in assuming she wouldn't be able to figure out what had happened and wouldn't want to do anything about it.

11

NO SYMPATHY FROM THE SHERIFF

The doors to the jail in the rear of the Silver Vein law office were wide open. Behind the floor-to-ceiling bars of her cell, Lil was a hugely interested but exasperated witness when Virginia came nervously to swear out a complaint.

The upset ranch-girl crimsoned from shame, trying to report in polite language to a leering Sheriff Hamish Howard that she'd been ravished by Dr François Guiscard.

Lil felt a deal of sympathy for her that Howard didn't. Anybody but him would have been moved by her despair.

In fact, Howard was downright opposed to taking any action and virtually said so. As always, it was too much effort. His attitude was that the alleged horse –

Guiscard – had already bolted. Moreover, Lil didn't doubt Howard was mindful that if he pursued the French doctor for this new crime, it would tend to lend credence to the somewhat similar allegations against him by herself.

This time Howard believed he had Lil sewn up – nailed 'good an' proper'. No way did he want any sidetracking that might let her off the hook.

'Sorry, missy,' he told Virginia. 'It ain't like yuh're presentin' any real evidence to back your charges. Supposin' yuh have bin – uh – something has happened to yuh. How'd any jury know it was Guiscard done it?'

'Because I would say so!' the distressed girl wailed. 'It hurt all night. Today I can still barely sit. I need to excuse myself every hour. He has damaged me!'

'Now hold your hosses. Him bein' a doc, he'd be sure to deny it. Make some explanation of how yuh're prob'ly mistaken. That'd end up bein' a case o' his word ag'inst your'n. Mebbe he'd say some other man did it. Or mebbe yuh invited him. . . . I figure it's another far-fetched story open to a lot o' readin's. Gals with wild claims are gittin' to be a glut in Silver Vein!'

Lil was no stranger to the clear acoustics of the office and jail. The place was built from Utah granite quarried from Little Cottonwood Canyon in Salt Lake County. Even a whisper sometimes seemed to bounce off the stone, amplified to a ringing declaration. Lil seethed as Howard rambled on and she learned his prime interest was in getting Virginia to drop her charges.

'Let word out o' what yuh says went on an' yuh'll be

ruined,' he said. 'No decent feller'll look at yuh ag'in, Miss Whitpath.'

Lil felt constrained to cut in.

'I can hear all what you're saying over there, Sheriff. I'm disgusted. As a lawdog you're a puppy with lots of yap and no bite!'

Howard swung in his cushioned swivel chair.

'Shuddup, Lil Goodnight! Yuh're in 'nough trouble o' your own. This gal needs good advice.'

'I can give her better than you!'

'Oh, yuh think so, do yuh?'

'Sure. She needs telling being a maiden ain't the only thing in a girl's life. You don't change as a person when you stop being one. There's nothing shows so someone can point at you and go, "You've lost it, how dare you!" Yes, it might hurt some today, but it's gotta happen one day. And after a few times with a decent man, she might know it for something good.'

It was Howard's turn to grow red in the face.

'Shuddup!' he roared again. 'What yuh say don't solve Miss Whitpath's predicament. If what she says is truth, she's a fallen woman.'

'Damn you, she ain't!' Lil snapped. 'If you weren't such a hard-nosed bastard as well as a lazy one, you'd let me out of here to track down the slimy, no-good doctor who deflowered her and bring him back to answer.'

'That ain't gonna happen, slut. Never! Yuh're in here till the judge passes sentence.'

'Sorry, Virginia,' Lil called, pointedly addressing the girl. 'You heard what the sheriff said. While I'm locked up, nobody's going to take care of Guiscard for us.

Nobody wearing a tin star anyways. So if you want help, you're looking in the wrong direction. The dirty doc'll get off scot-free.'

'Hush your mouth, I said,' Howard rapped. 'Yuh got no case against the Frenchie.'

This contemptuously declared, he turned to the red-faced Virginia.

'Miss Whitpath, for the sake o' your reputation an' your folks, yuh should keep quiet, yuh unnerstand? Your uncle an' aunt raised yuh jest like they was your own parents – jest like any other kid in Silver Vein. Yuh can't repay 'em by lettin' it be spread round their li'l gal ain't the sweet, innocent thing she was no more. That's she's had herself a tumble. . . .'

Virginia nodded, lowering her face in shame.

With the sheriff's back to her, Lil began a frantic bid to convey a message to the other girl in dumb show. But would she see? Would she understand?

Lil formed her fingers to make a gun. She also pointed to her belt, to the exact place where normally she would carry a Colt in a holster.

'Remember the warnin',' Howard lectured. 'I feel kinda sorry for yuh in a way. An' mebbe I don't blame yuh fer comin' here, but it sure would turn a bad business worse if yuh pressed the complaint outside these walls.'

Lil carried on making her signs, sure that Virginia had noticed her strange antics, though sensibly for once she wasn't letting on.

Lil indicated the gun she was making out of the fingers of her left hand by pointing at it with her right forefinger. She then jabbed the same forefinger toward the wall on her left – the wall dividing her cell from Lucky M'Cline's.

Did Virginia get the message?

When the distressed girl left, shoulders slumped and dragging her feet, Lil still didn't really know she had. She could only continue to catch at straws.

The message was, of course, that Virginia should bring Lucky a gun. She'd previously been allowed to visit her old sweetheart, bringing him biscuits and fruit in her basket. Lucky was a likeable cuss. Half the girls in the county were secretly in love with the rogue. Maybe Virginia had been hoping to win him back since Lil was wholly blackened as a bank robber and a cold-blooded murderer. Or maybe she'd resented the pair – Lucky and Lil – being in jail cells that were side by side.

Sheriff Howard hadn't tried to stop her bringing the small gifts of edibles. Prisoners had to be fed out of the county purse and basic meals were brought in from the Traveller's Rest hotel kitchen. It galled Howard having to pay for the stuff. Fact was, he earmarked for personal luxuries the lion's share of the fees and taxes he gathered as a right of his office. If some do-gooder with a soft heart saw fit to feed a prisoner, why, that meant less grub was needed from elsewhere, didn't it?

Lil figured Howard's meanness with the revenues would help dull any suspicion. But that was one or two steps ahead. First, Virginia had to have understood what she was required to bring and have the spunk to do it.

She sat down on the hard bunk's thin straw mattress to wait and hope.

*

It was a full day before Virginia appeared again in the sheriff's office. Lil hoped she'd spent the time well, acquiring a suitable firearm. She did have her basket on her arm, its contents promisingly covered by a red and white gingham cloth.

'How'd yuh be now, Miss Whitpath?' Howard greeted her, doing a bad job of hiding a knowing smirk.

'Poorly, Mr Howard. I'm sore and I have constant cramps, but I'm sure you don't really need to know, since you can't – won't – do anything about righting the wrong I've suffered.'

He shrugged. 'Aw, well, what matters is yuh've seen sense in stayin' close-mouthed. Thar' ain't no scuttlebutt around town 'bout devilish docs. We'll keep it that way, won't we? Brung your ol' pal more tucker, I see. Dunno why yuh still bother settin' your cap. He's jest fiddlefooted Texan trash.'

'I don't wish to discuss it with you, Sheriff.'

Howard jeered at the dismissive tone.

'Time now yuh dropped the Miss Prim 'n' Proper line, ain't it? But go ahead. Yuh can shove the stuff through the bars. Mebbe he'll give yuh a kiss, though I guess – bein' a woman an' all – it'll jest make yuh hanker fer the rest!'

He laughed at his crude witticism but made no move to lift his boots off his scarred desktop or to shift his fat ass off his cushioned chair.

Lil growled in her throat at his insensitivity, yet said nothing to draw any attention to the cells and their two inmates. Howard would keep . . . hopefully till Lucky M'Cline was armed and he was being obliged to set them free.

'Guess we can trust a *good* gal like yuhself not to pull no tricks,' Howard said, and began building himself a smoke.

Virginia came back to where the jail's three cells ranged in a row fronted by bars incorporating their heavy doors. She spoke with Lucky in whispers and Lil hoped Howard would think they were saying sweet nothings. She also hoped that they were much more.

Finally, Virginia moved away, with words of farewell that were audible.

'Enjoy the cookies, Lucky. And please don't forget to come see me sometime.'

Lil's heart leapt. That sounded like Virginia expected him to be on the loose. Don't say anything more, she begged silently, else Howard will get suspicious.

But the lazy sheriff only laughed. 'Sometime won't be in a long time, missy. He ain't got no choice in it. Why don't yuh fergit 'im? Experienced young lady like yuhself could please a lotta other fellers!'

Virginia could stand no more of his heavy humour. With a kind of exasperated sob, she left in a rush, leaving only her quick footsteps tapping along the plank sidewalk. And, Lil could only trust, the means to freedom with Lucky M'Cline. . . .

That afternoon, when Howard had fallen into a siesta, Lucky M'Cline came to the front corner of his cell and called quietly.

'Lil, Virginia brung me the gun, like she says you asked. What do we do?'

Lil was relieved at the confirmation that her plan was working so far, but she knew the most difficult part was still to be accomplished. How best to work it?

After swift consideration, she said *sotto voce*, 'Listen, Lucky, hold the gun out through your bars, as far to the right as you can, and I'll reach out through mine and see if I can get it in here. Then we'll work it like this. . . .'

That evening, after the daytime sounds of the town outside had gone quiet and darkness was falling, Lucky yelled out, 'Sheriff – hey, Sheriff! You gotta help me! Come quickly!'

Howard was looking forward to handing over to his deputy, Sly Connor, due to take the night shift in another half-hour.

'Eh. . . ? What the hell's goin' on? Less of the racket, M'Cline!'

Lucky groaned convincingly and made noises like he was throwing up.

'Gawd, Sheriff – I been poisoned! That damn gal brought me poisoned cookies! I'm gonna die! Oh, oh – it's burnin' m' throat an' stomach . . . bring me water!'

Grabbing a clinking bunch of keys and a lantern, Howard let out a gusty sigh of annoyance.

'Shit! I shoulda never trusted that prissy li'l goody-goody! She done it t' spite me, I know!'

Lucky collapsed to the stone floor of his cell with what sounded like a ponderous slap, but was achieved mostly by smacking his open palms on the flags. He began retching again.

'Aw, aw! I'm dyin'! Yeeurgh!'

'All right, all right! Keep the shirt on your back!'

Howard had put down the lantern and was thrusting the key into the lock on Lucky's cell door, when he heard an ominous, metallic click. He looked up to see that Lil was pointing a long-barrelled .44 Colt at him from the adjacent cell.

'Keep going, Sheriff! Do your stuff with the key, then open up this one, too. The gun's cocked and my finger's tight on the trigger. A squeeze and you'll be blown away. I'm a ruthless murderer of bank tellers, remember?'

Howard shook his head disbelievingly.

'What in hell. . . ? Man, where'd yuh git that thing?'

'Don't fuss your dumb brain, law puppy! You heard what I said. Just do it.'

Howard saw the steely glint in Lil's grey eyes. Never the bravest of men, he decided promptly to give her no argument.

Lil emerged from her cell as Lucky got up from the floor in his.

'Hey! Yuh're sick, M'Cline!' Howard flared.

'Not any more he's not,' Lil said.

Smiling grimly, the kid from Texas drawled, 'But you're gonna be!'

He swung a punch at Howard's dropped jaw that sent him, stunned, to the floor.

'Ouch!' Lil said. 'Go easy, Lucky. We ain't looking to give anybody a real reason to hang us.'

'Sure, Lil, but the bastard ain't the strong an' silent type. He's sure gonna have a shuck in his snoot an' won't let us ride outa town alive if'n he's got a busy lip.'

When the half-conscious sheriff regained his full senses, he found himself behind the office desk set on his cushioned swivel chair. He was in just his longjohns and had been tied to his favourite workplace with strips of cloth torn from his own shirt.

He could utter only muffled curses because he'd also been gagged.

Misfit Lil and Lucky M'Cline were nowhere in sight or hearing.

12

SON OF A BADMAN

After Lil and Lucky had retrieved their mounts at gunpoint from the livery stable, and before they hightailed it out of the Silver Vein country, they called in at the Whitpath ranch.

'We're relying on you to help, Mr Whitpath,' Lil said. 'Sheriff Howard hasn't given Virginia or us a square deal.'

George Whitpath had greatly revised his opinions of François Guiscard, Hamish Howard and Purity Wadsworth. Only preservation of the good name of his niece had stayed him from action to expose their joint sins, derelictions and misrepresentations.

He was glad to wish Lucky and Lil success in their planned hunt for the evil French mesmerist and provisioned them for what could be a long trail. He also pressed on them what money he could spare as a small rancher.

'You won't get far going half-shod.'

'You're just about exactly the best doggone square-shooter I met anywhere a-tall,' Lucky told him.

Virginia, sniffing a mite and dabbing at her eyes with a handkerchief, could offer Lil no information on where Guiscard might have taken himself and the bank loot.

'They say he put himself and all his bags on the Green River stage the same day he attacked me. He bought a ticket to ride a train.'

'To where?'

'No one could say.'

'Damn! The trains go all over from Green River,' Lil said. 'The Denver, Rio Grande railroad links with the Union Pacific north of Salt Lake City, or with the Atchison, Topeka an' Santa Fe in Colorado. Then, he could've headed east into Kansas through Dodge City, or south into New Mexico, through Santa Fe. He could be in old Mexico by now!'

Virginia moaned. 'And the villain has left me maybe with some dreaded illness, or worse. I still hurt.'

Lucky said, 'Go git some ephedra plant, darlin'. In the Big Bend country they swear by it for them sorta complaints. You boil the leaves an' drink it. Hereabouts, in Utah, I do recall it's called Mormon tea.'

'Oh!' Virginia exclaimed with a louder, shocked sob. 'That's exactly the kind of thing a drifter like you would know about, isn't it?'

'Lord God!' Virginia's aunt choked. 'Why did our family have to be visited by such scandal?'

Lucky tried to look sheepish, then worsened the

situation by making a promise that Lil, and probably each of the Whitpaths, knew he wouldn't keep.

'I'll be back, Virginia. I'll take a paralysed oath on it. Why, you're my faithful ol' stand-by and I won't cabbage on you.'

But Lil knew he was a kid who'd gone to the gates and wouldn't do for Virginia to tie to. He was fun, but he'd committed all the vices known to man or boy and was unreliable. Marriage to a tame homebody like Virginia would never appeal to him. Come back here? Once they'd lit out, Lil didn't reckon he ever would.

But for the moment, he was the only partner she had, and she thought she had the means to keep him on her side. The moon had risen and the time came for goodbyes to the Whitpaths. He took the trail beside her for Green River without looking back at the jealous hurt in Virginia's face as she stared after the vanishing, fugitive riders.

They knew they would be travelling fast and Lil would have liked to take second horses with them, carrying loaded pack saddles and capable of being alternated with their first mounts when they tired. With regular switches, they could have pushed the horses harder.

Lucky's eyes were bright with the anticipation of adventure and devilry, but Lil recognized they had a difficult job of tracking ahead of them. It wouldn't be the normal one, at which she was no novice. There'd be no stopping to read sign; tracks in the dust; scrapes on rocks; broken twigs at the sides of narrow, timbered trails. Guiscard could be on the move from settlement to settlement, town to town, by rail and stageline. Meanwhile, his pursuers would be having to rest their horses and themselves.

As jailbreakers, they'd have to be careful how and where they showed themselves; to make their necessary enquiries circumspectly. Even Hamish Howard was liable to make the effort in due course to send out word, far and wide by wire, describing his escaped prisoners.

All the while Lil was troubled by the daunting aspects of the mission, they pounded the dark road, away from Silver Vein and the wild country she knew as home . . . and which to her was like a safe backyard typical to a young woman of her age and time.

Two weeks elapsed between the time Lil and Lucky broke out of Hamish Howard's cells and when Jackson Farraday returned from the Henry Mountains.

'Lilian Goodnight robbed the bank?' he questioned, disbelieving what he heard.

The civilian scout and guide had gone directly to Fort Dennis, standing square, solid and familiar behind its massive log stockade out on the flats yonder from Silver Vein. His intention had been to advise the army that his services were again available.

But in a sparsely furnished office in the clinically stark, stone-built administration block, Lieutenant Michael Covington was brimming over with the news of the shocking events surrounding Misfit Lil. He was well aware that the Goodnight girl regarded him, Jackson, as a mentor.

Jackson was nigh on twice Lil's age and liked to think his interest in Lil was, in fact, rather like that of a father – Lil's real father having been shunned by the girl since she hadn't appreciated his attempts to make a young lady of her.

Contrariwise, Lil hero-worshipped Jackson and would yield everything to him; he had only to relax his guard and allow it. Also, she represented to despise 'Mike' Covington, with whom she was more of an age, mocking his West Point precision and rectitude at every opportunity.

For these complex reasons, and the growing list of episodes that had arisen out of them, Covington was a committed critic of Ben Goodnight's harum-scarum daughter and delighted in passing on the news to Jackson that she was well on the way to a deserved bad end.

'Yes!' Covington clipped. 'Robbed the bank. Later, she escaped from jail, attacking Sheriff Howard and leaving him tied to his desk chair in his longjohns.'

The young lieutenant plainly took the last very seriously, so Jackson had to hide the smile that threatened to curve the lips above his neat beard. He lowered his head and ran a strong, bronzed hand over his flowing, sun-bleached hair.

'Ah well,' Jackson said, 'I doubt that was too inconvenient. We both know the sheriff prefers to be sitting in his chair than anything else – a saddle, for instance.'

'It was a disgrace, however! She cocked a snoot at the elected law in cahoots with a Texas grub-line rider – a fellow of the desperado stripe, now known to have a black record in other territories.'

'Oh? Who was this?'

Covington replied with cold distaste. 'A fellow prisoner with whom she'd previously been sharing her blankets, I hear. One Robert, or Lucky, M'Cline. He'd previously shot and wounded a Negro trooper, part of a detachment garrisoned here to aid our campaign against the renegade Indian Angry-fist.'

But Jackson was murmuring thoughtfully, 'M'Cline . . . M'Cline. From Texas. I know that name!'

'You do?'

Covington should not have been surprised. Jackson was a man of wide interests and knowledge. He'd been all over the frontier West. In the past, he'd hunted buffalo and supplied meat for railroad construction workers. He'd also carried dispatches through hostile Indian country. He was a living reminder of the pathfinders who'd blazed western trails earlier in the century. An educated man, he reputedly spoke seven languages plus an assortment of Indian dialects. And he'd been west of the Pecos River and through the Texas Big Bend country more than once.

Jackson explained.

'They say many *hombres* in those vast and colourful, wide-open spaces are tough as a boot and twice as high. But old Bad John M'Cline was the worst and often drunk. He was a mean and quarrelsome man, always on the prod. And in West Texas, folks get vexed easily with such a feller, specially if he's always showing out. A man may talk big, but he's not to talk idly and dishonestly.

To brag is one thing; to be a complete braggart is another. Combined with a vicious temper, it's unpardonable,'

Covington nodded. 'It's not tolerated in men in uniform. Discipline includes self-discipline and is everything.'

Jackson smiled faintly, then pressed on.

'Bad John's sprees always ended up with him treeing the town where he lived. After he'd killed three men for no good cause, he was ambushed and killed by a vigilante group that had grown tired and fearful of his ugly temper and his readiness to do mischief with a gun. They lay in wait in a jumble of rocks and toppled him from his saddle with rifles.'

'And who was this Bad John?' Covington asked, though he could guess the answer.

'John M'Cline had a son named Robert.'

'So he was our Lucky M'Cline's father! That I can easily accept. The boy is a born hellion. Mixed with an unreformed minx like Lilian Goodnight, he's pure poison. 'Less they're brought here to be hanged, Silver Vein is well rid of them.'

'Isn't that a little harsh?'

'Indeed no! The Goodnight girl shot dead a teller who'd witnessed her committing the robbery. She's a murderess.'

Jackson frowned. He definitely didn't believe it.

'Do tell more.'

Covington responded to the request by giving the details, as far as they were known, of Ossie Caldeen's death. He finished by roundly denouncing Misfit Lil.

'Her character is blacker than ever. You must wash your hands of her, as I have. She has gone too far this time, turning into a completely amoral criminal. According to Sheriff Howard, she put up a ridiculous defence that Dr François Guiscard, a celebrated French mesmerist whom her father had hired to cure her misbehaviour, made her rob the bank in a trance. To boot, that the niece of rancher George Whitpath, who was acting as a nurse, had been placed under a similar influence.'

Jackson clutched at the offered straw of mitigation.

'Hypnosis. . . . What does Miss Whitpath say?'

'A deluded child in the care of her aunt and uncle! But a respectable young lady who was plainly led astray by Misfit Lil. A polite veil has been drawn over her testimony, I understand.'

Jackson said shrewdly, 'So she, too, accuses Dr Guiscard. What does he say?'

'Given his failure with Misfit Lil, which surprised no one of good sense, Dr Guiscard has since left town. He probably knows nothing of the preposterous allegations that have been made against him. A bank robbery under hypnosis: perfectly absurd, Mr Farraday!'

'You don't believe in hypnosis, Lieutenant?'

'Not to any extravagant degree. Lil Goodnight's claims are of a kind that might be dreamed up by an over-imaginative girl who'd read about the tricks of stage hypnotists back East.'

Jackson did not know instantly how he could argue on that score. He shrugged.

'Hmm. . . . I don't know what I can say there.

Hypnosis was used during the War Between the States by army field-doctors. It has been supplanted only because we now have the hypodermic needle and the chemical anaesthetics ether and chloroform.'

Covington didn't relent.

'If Miss Goodnight could prove her case was sound with scientific evidence, why did she break out of jail and go on the dodge?'

'Because she didn't know she'd be able to get that proof,' Jackson suggested.

'Too right. The robbery was witnessed by the Reverend Titus Fisher, you know. Science is apt to be on shaky ground when it challenges religion.'

Jackson chose to ignore Covington's reliance on the local representative of the church.

'And Lil could scarcely count on Hamish Howard to investigate for her. He would have had no interest at all in establishing the truth. Nothing ever does interest him that isn't easy – or doesn't better his personal comfort and status.'

'It should have been thrashed out in a court of law.'

'Under the auspices of an overworked circuit judge who'd no doubt have ridden a far piece to reach Silver Vein. Lil would've been mindful of horrific newspaper reports of notorious hanging judges reaching prompt and quirky decisions. Unbiased local jurors would be hard to find, too. Many folks – especially those in business – would happily collude with the prosecution to appease the likes of Miss Purity Wadsworth and her cronies.'

'I can see we shall never see eye to eye on this, Mr Farraday.'

'Maybe so. Knowing how Lil's mind works – as we should after close on a half-dozen experiences of it – I figure she'll be somewhere on the trail of Dr Guiscard.'

'Heaven help them both,' Covington said insincerely and dismissively.

'I don't think I'll leave it to such higher power, Lieutenant.'

Jackson had decided, after only a mite of soul-searching, that he must ride out straight away in pursuit of Lil and her new companion. Knowing the Texan kid's ancestry, he also figured Covington was right in that Lil and Lucky M'Cline made a bad combination. The pair were doomed to run into trouble for sure. Their instincts would be to shoot their way out of it, but they'd only shoot themselves into worse.

Jackson feared that on what was effectively an outlaw trail the young M'Cline would quickly go to bad. The breed would come out and he'd become old Bad John M'Cline to a T.

Would he be in time to save Lil Goodnight from her folly in choosing to side a reckless young man liable to turn out a blowhard and bully like his father?

13

GUISCARD'S NEW LAIR

By Misfit Lil's reckoning she and Lucky M'Cline had travelled some 400 miles, crossing the border into Colorado and threading a path by way of high passes across the Rocky Mountains.

'This ain't my kinda country,' Lucky complained. 'I like it wide and open.'

'Be thankful it ain't winter,' Lil told him. 'Consider how grand it is, like the Wasatch canyons, though considerable more of it.'

The mountains around them were sculpted by glaciers, producing impressively rugged outcrops and vistas of sweeping upland scenery. Lil knew that such a landscape would be subject to a heavy covering of snow in winter. Similar places in Utah's Wasatch Range received 500 inches of snowfall a year. Their journey had taken them nearly two weeks. Some days they made forty miles; others less. They dared not press their horses harder and Lil was finding Lucky, who was not long on patience, increasingly testy. There was no fun for him in what they were doing. It kept him out of the hands of the law, but his interest in Lil's quest to find and wreak vengeance on Dr François Guiscard was minimal.

The summer days were pleasant, with high sun and high temperatures. At night though, temperatures dropped hugely into the mid-fifties and lower. Always camping out, they wrapped themselves closely together in their blankets. Lucky was no way averse to the arrangement. Every night he availed himself vigorously of the intimacy it facilitated.

Lil wondered if he might privately view the pleasure-taking as compensation for his daytime boredom; for humouring her in her mission. Not once did they notice the cold. But though Lil never withheld her favours – she equally enjoyed their warming exertions – Lucky grumbled that it would be good sometime to spend a handful of the money Whitpath had given them on a night in a tavern.

Lil, who wisely held the purse, was wary of the suggestion. By now, dodgers on them could be posted all over. Too, she feared that in a tavern Lucky would waste their funds on liquor and his loose, drunken bragging would draw attention to them.

Moreover, the crowded accommodations in these primitive, scattered places frequently entailed sharing of rooms, even beds, with strangers. It was customary to sleep fully clothed, after removing boots, so such conditions didn't inevitably promote promiscuity and exchange of confidences, but Lil nonetheless dismissed them as dangerous.

In a rowdy little mining town known as Columbia, they learned that a French doctor was causing a minor stir some hundred miles north-west in a place called Tribune Springs. Their informant, a drummer for a hardware wholesaler they met while shopping in a general store for fresh food, told them the 'foreign doc' was setting up a rural sanatorium for disturbed womenfolk.

'It'll be a refuge for ailing ladies driven to distraction and more by city life. Their kinfolk – if'n they're wealthy enough to pay the fees – will send them there rather than to the regular insane asylums.'

Lucky made to speak. Lil was sure he was going to divulge that they were looking for such a doctor, name of Guiscard, and he was a rogue. She elbowed him, apparently accidentally, in the ribs.

'How interesting! We'd like to hear more,' she said, keen to capitalize on their stroke of luck.

The loquacious drummer revealed that the sanatorium was grandly sporting the name Arcadia Park.

'I figure he got his notions offa General Palmer who calls his place at Colorado Springs Fountain Colony, though Palmer's establishment is for the tubercular gentility.'

It appeared the French doctor had bought the deed to the property, previously going under the mundane name of Pickford's, from a well-to-do cattle rancher who'd made a bad call on its possibilities. After an unusually harsh winter, the cattleman had been anxious to head south with the remnants of his herd for a warmer climate. He'd wanted to quit the palatial ranch house, complete with Grecian columns gracing its porch, which he'd had built for his wife and family by specialist tradesmen brought in from Denver and as far away as New Orleans.

'The Frenchie is planning on special exhibitions of his cures, they do say,' the drummer added. 'Entertainments, sort of, to help fill the coffers for further expansion. Seems like in the salons of Paris, it's the way things used to be done regularly. This medico is going to revive the practice.'

Lil said politely, 'Thank you, sir. Maybe we'll go take a look-see for ourselves.'

They left the store with Lucky laughing at her.

'Damn right we will! Guiscard prob'ly bought the Pickford's layout with the money you stole from the bank.'

They rode out of Columbia's isolated box canyon and made good time through the pure, dry mountain air to Tribune Springs, reaching it in two days by dint of long spells of trotting and cantering.

The small township of Tribune Springs should have been a showcase of an emergent centre, served by a narrow-gauge railroad from points east and greater civilization. The Utes had been moved to a reservation. It had new brick, pine and log houses huddled together and a bustling downtown of sorts with a range of stores, two blacksmith shops, a livery barn, a bank, a hotel and three saloons.

Lil decided to put up their horses at the livery.

'Rebel is looking tolerable gaunted from the long trail. I don't like that.'

Her trusty grey had galloped up and down hill, never missed his foot on the roughest ground and needed only the mildest words and touches of her heels for encouragement.

She told the hostler, 'I'd like him rubbed down and given some grain. He hasn't had any for a spell.'

Lucky resented the expenditure. He'd had other ideas now they planned to stop in a town.

'I figured to have m'self a time,' he said.

Like the cowboys who worked the ranches in the area, for Lucky coming to town meant hitting the saloons and other establishments for rest, recreation and socializing, though few women were in evidence on the settlement's streets and newcomers were quickly made aware that Tribune Springs was under the tight control of Marshal Wal Deegan.

Deegan ruled with the proverbial iron fist; more exactly iron in his fist: a big Smith & Wesson .44 with an eight-inch barrel. They received the information from chat with the livery's old hostler – bent by time, rheumatism and cynicism – that he used it to shoot or pistol whip the recalcitrant and rowdy into line. Deegan was arrogant and a bully.

'Sounds like he's as bad a lot as Sheriff Howard back home,' Lil said to Lucky a day later.

'Nope. He's smarter an' he works hard at it. He collects hefty insurance from all the town's businesses, for their protection.'

'Yeah?' Lil said drily.

'This Deegan ain't no Hamish Howard. He's tough, knows how to run the show an' can count on twentysome men to make what he says stick.'

Lil had conceded to Lucky's demands for 'a taste of luxury' and a bed indoors. At two dollars a day, they'd taken a room at the hotel, where she was lying low, reckoning Lucky would be less apt to be noticed on his lonesome, being little different from many other saddle tramps drifting western trails.

She correctly figured Lucky was looking for new excitements and Deegan, his hardcase crew and the respect they were afforded, all impressed him. She suspected her own attractions, though she still made them freely available, were beginning to pall for Lucky.

She'd caught glimpses of Deegan, strutting down the centre of his town's main street just as though he did in truth own the place. He had wide shoulders and blond hair that curled from under the band of a black, bell-crowned hat. He was big – of a similar imposing height to Jackson Farraday.

A sigh came to Lil's lips when she thought of Jackson. Was being with Lucky a disloyalty to the man she really admired?

Lucky, like she'd heard others note, was a likeable fellow. He came across with rugged charm – tanned brown face and blue eyes. Even when narrowed and grimed with dust, the eyes were bright and alert and possessing a hint of lazy humour. He had generous, well-shaped lips that knew how to kiss, and a square chin with a cleft. Everything about him spoke of open, healthy spaces, and his voice held the lazy drawl which proved him a native of Texas.

Those were the good points, but at bottom was he any damn good to a girl with a firm purpose in being here?

Well, of course he was. If he admired Deegan and his hirelings, it would be easy for him to rub shoulders with them and learn what she needed to know about Guiscard's operations here. It was plain these had to be with the connivance of Marshal Deegan. Everything was. And Guiscard would be able to pay Deegan his percentage. It looked like he'd already invested some of the bank loot into a new racket that promised to produce ongoing profits.

Lil put it to Lucky.

'I'd like you to mix with Marshal Deegan's crowd and find out all you can for me about Pickford's.'

Lucky was nothing loath. He didn't share her contempt for Deegan's paid gunfighter types, who frequented the saloons where the air rang with ribaldry and profanity and the clientele was entirely masculine. Lil had nothing against these places – and knew how to look after herself in them – but as a stranger here and a fugitive, she didn't want to be made conspicuous by the bother of proving it.

'Sweetheart,' Lucky drawled, 'gimme some o' Whitpath's dinero to buy the drinks, an' it's as good as done.'

In the event, Lucky did more than Lil asked for, which led to an exchange of cross words, but not before he'd reported with enthusiasm that Dr François Guiscard was in business at his Arcadia Park and had the support of his new friends, Deegan's toughs, and the local citizenry in general.

'Thar's considerable int'rest an' amazement. Like that drummer in Columbia said, normal folks go to Pickford's to watch Guiscard work on the afflicted. They call 'em hysterics an' the doc lies 'em on electro-medico-celestial beds.'

'Electro-horsefeathers!' Lil said scornfully.

' 'Cept it works an' them smooth hides from the East talk about their visions fer ever'body to hear.'

'Hallucinations!' Lil said. 'Such fooling ain't right.'

Lucky shrugged. 'Ain't got no argument with none of it m'self. Deegan's boys talked my arm off. The doc told a patient she was at the Pearly Gates an' she described the Virgin Mary, the saints an' angels. Another, a God-fearin', standoffish mother, was made to take on, turn about, the manner of a priest, a general an' a French actress. The actress was also a courtesan mighty free with cussin'! The folks who paid to watch the ladies in their trances had a fine ol' laugh.'

'I'd call it a disgusting exhibition.'

'Thought yuh wanted to know jest how the wind's a-blowin' an' the dust's a-flyin'.'

'I did.'

'Wal, yuh ain't heard it all yet,' Lucky said, reacting to her stiffness. 'Seems Deegan's got room in his crew for one more – an' I aim to be it! Thataway, I get inside

Pickford's to see the fun fer free with my own eyes. Better, these hysterics sometimes need restrainin' an' Deegan's fellers git called to ride herd on 'em, chousin' 'em back to their rooms fer calmin' down. An' a bronc-buster like me sure knows how to break a mockey!'

Lucky's glee made Lil feel sick. On the trail, away from drink and other men, he'd been different. Now his bad streak was coming out again. She'd been one of Guiscard's hapless victims herself. In making it plain he had no qualms about abusing the sanatorium's patients, he also showed he'd gone rotten.

She realized she was tired of Lucky's brags. At best, he'd been all mouth and gunsmoke from the time he'd cut loose at the clock in McHendry's saloon in Silver Vein. Also, she'd known from the start – same as Virginia Whitpath hadn't, setting her cap at him – that Lucky was no one-girl man. From what had been learned, Deegan's bunch saw Pickford's as their private cat house. And Lucky was hot to join them.

It was an appalling situation but wouldn't be seen as such by a society that didn't want to know. Insanity was regarded by most of the families it struck as shameful. Husbands, fathers and other kin locked the afflicted away in asylums. They didn't care how the unfortunate sufferers were treated as long as they were out of sight of the people who knew them. Thus the disgrace was avoided. A retreat in the Rockies fitted the bill better than other solutions . . . the guilty relatives could fool themselves they'd acted compassionately, especially if they were allowed to remain ignorant of what really happened there.

Lucky appeared lost to Lil's cause, which was to expose Guiscard and bring him to justice. He had little interest in it. Nor could she keep him sweet by playing on his male desires. They weren't alone together in the wilderness any more. His whole interest in that direction was apparently caught by the novel and alluring hunting-ground at Pickford's. But maybe he could still be of use to her. . . .

By morning, after sleeping on the problem, she had it figured out. She would encourage Lucky to be part of Deegan's outfit after all.

'I thought you was mad at me about that.'

'Who was mad?'

'It sounded like you was.'

'Well, maybe I was then. Now I need to get inside Guiscard's sanatorium disguised as a patient, is all. Do you think you could fix that?'

Lucky was startled.

'I think you're crazy! I don't know. . . .'

'I do! There must be evidence in that big, swank ranch house that Guiscard got his money from Silver Vein. The only way for me to find it is to get inside and go hunt.'

14

MISPLACED TRUST?

Lil waited behind the cover of a pile of timber ties and a clump of brush on the edge of the railroad depot sidings. Unfamiliarly, she was dressed in a brown, broadcloth dress embroidered with red and green flowers, a black travelling cape and a black silk bonnet. Her financial straits were now very serious. The purchases had reduced the Whitpath money from its last few dollars to cents. This was going to have to work!

A party of new women patients was due to arrive in Tribune Springs on the morning train. From town, Deegan's men would convey them to Dr Guiscard's sanatorium by a mud wagon, which had seats in rows and a canvas canopy to give shade.

The business was still in its early days and, as far as Lucky had been able to ascertain, the arrangements were informal, no one quite knowing exactly how many women were due. It seemed to hang uncertainly on the patients' conditions and the circumstances at their places of origin. And payment of Dr Guiscard's fees, of course.

On time, a smoke-belching, ash-spewing locomotive clattered and clanked into the arrogantly named 'station' that was mostly a yard overgrown with weeds. It pulled four cars and a caboose. The loco's big brass bell tolled and steam screamed through its whistle. The cars were one for passengers, two flatbed wagons, with freight covered by lashed-down canvas, and a boxcar.

When the train passed her, Lil saw only a handful of passengers, all male. Heart beating a little faster, she peered round the ties to watch.

A few loafers curious to see what the train had shipped in clustered round as it chugged to a hissing halt. Deegan's four men, including Lucky, pushed past them and stood not by the passenger car but in front of the closed-in boxcar.

A peak-capped conductor left the caboose and went to the boxcar. He released the locking bar and slid back the door with a rumble along its tracks and climbed inside, calling orders.

About a dozen women were helped down from the car's dark maw into the arms of Deegan's waiting crew. Stood on their feet, they looked unsteady as though they had cramps in their legs, which was likely the case, depending on how uncomfortably they'd been confined in their boxcar berths.

They also blinked and screwed up their eyes against

the sudden light of a strong sun in a very blue sky. Lil noted all their faces were much paler than her own. She hoped that bleaching her hair and changing her attire were adequate moves to disguise her identity from Dr Guiscard.

On the other hand, the women's pale faces could signal not so much indoor living or mental sickness as minds filled with apprehension and fright. She'd seen the same look in the eyes of small critters, like chipmunks and squirrels, caught in traps.

The women were shepherded and hauled toward the waiting mud wagon by Deegan's men, Lucky among them. Lil had to give the Texan credit. He did nothing that was brutal while also doing nothing to betray himself as being less committed to the job than his companions. But he had to be sitting as much on the edge of his nerves as she was.

Lil didn't reckon any man who tried to put one across Wal Deegan was allowed to live long.

Subtly, Lucky contributed to the muddle as the fearful women – still stiff and confused from the rigors of riding a train hidden away in the darkness and discomfort of a boxcar – were ushered toward another stage of their gruelling journey. Lucky pushed his charge in the direction of the pile of ties and clump of brush. Lil slipped out from cover and joined them.

'The hell with it!' Lucky said. 'Stop draggin' them feet, ladies. Thisaway! Yuh wanna be left behind?'

As a trio they merged into the main party, Lil imitating the women's shambling gait and air of distraction. Or was it despair?

She wondered if some of them had been drugged, sedated.

'Sun,' one of them mumbled to no one in particular. 'Haven't seen the sun since I don't know when.'

'Won't see a whole lot more of it neither, ma'am, where yuh're goin',' a tough lipped back, snickering. His companions laughed coarsely.

As soon as the women, including Lil, had been loaded on to the wagon and seated, the men went to their saddled horses, hitched to a fence close by, and swung up.

The wagon driver slapped his horses' backs with the reins, urging them across the tracks. Deegan's riders fell in and formed a tight escort for the last leg of the women's journey to Arcadia Park.

Lil didn't like the dangers that waited in ambush for sure along the unblazed trail she was taking, but it was too late to turn back now.

What had gotten into her, thinking she could pull off this wild plan?

The drive took the best part of an hour. Most of the women stared blankly at the passing scenery. The loneliness of pine-dotted grass hills, rugged with great, strewn rocks and bounded by white-peaked, tooth-edged mountain ranges, was probably completely new and intimidating. Perhaps in their moments of lucidity the better informed among them would be consoled by remembrance that the climate of Colorado was considered the finest in North America.

Lil had read that consumptives, asthmatics,

dyspeptics and sufferers from nervous diseases were brought here in hundreds if not thousands. The air was rarefied and dry; in the summer months, sunshine was bright and almost constant. She and Lucky had slept comfortably out of doors on the trail across the border from Utah.

But she also knew that the women seated around her in the mud wagon were about to fall into the grasp of a charlatan. Dr François Guiscard was unlikely to effect any marvellous cures. Their relatives would be fleeced, as her father had been, and Guiscard would exploit any personal talents or attributes they had for his own purposes, just as he had done with Virginia and her.

The isolated Arcadia Park proved to be situated in an open valley with the former ranch-owner's grand house sitting impressively on a wide bench overlooking it.

Lil realized how ideal it might have first looked to Dr Guiscard, seeking a property where he could conduct his experiments and grow his wealth out of the world's view.

The mud wagon swept up to the imposing front porch with its Grecian columns – and there he was.

Dr Guiscard, his mane of silver hair seeming to glisten in the sunlight, was smartly dressed in striped trousers, black coat, wing collar and a flowing cravat. He made no move to come down from the porch and welcome his new patients. But Lil felt his eyes – those menacing, dark eyes – running over them, assessing the prospects.

By the time the women had disembarked from the wagon, he was gone.

The party was conducted into the house by Deegan's gang and several Spanish people of both sexes whom Lil took to be Guiscard's domestic staff.

They were taken to rooms lined with bunks which were euphemistically called dormitories. In fact, they were more crowded than the typical cattle-country bunkhouse, being designed as family bedrooms maybe for three or four children at most. Lil wondered how many more patients were housed in the big, long structure across a yard and corral that at a guess had originally been quarters for Pickford's hands.

With the cramped living conditions alone, she wouldn't want to waste any time in making her next move. Moreover, she wasn't confident her disguised identity would fool Dr Guiscard on close or prolonged inspection.

Although most of the arrivals seemed content to sleep, various women were summoned to meet the doctor during the course of the afternoon. Luckily, Lil wasn't included. She didn't know what paperwork had been delivered with the party, but obviously there would be none on her, which could lead to awkward questions.

That evening, in an outside privy, Lil took out a Colt revolver from under her skirt, cleaned and oiled it. When she came back to the dormitory, she laid it under her pillow. She resolved to keep awake.

During the night she planned to explore the house she'd infiltrated.

When the moon had risen and its light was filtering into the dormitory around the drawn blinds, Lil acted. She replaced the Colt in its holster under her skirt, which she'd not removed, and dropped from her bunk to the floor. She slumped to the floor, clutching her belly, groaning.

'What is wrong, *señorita*?' whispered the fat woman assigned as the room's nurse. Or guard.

'*S-sorry. . . . Me disculpo.* I – I'm sick, from the travel, I think. I need to go to the privy. I think I might throw up.'

Lil made retching noises.

'*Madre de Dios*! You must not make a mess in here!' the woman said, visualizing the cleaning up that might be required of her. 'Take yourself out pronto!'

Lil went, as quickly as would be feasible for a person with stomach gripes. But once around a corner in the passage outside, she moved lightning fast.

She eased open three doors before she found the room she was looking for: one furnished as an office. She slipped in and closed the door behind her. Promising. . . . More so when she came to a desk with locked drawers.

Seconds ticked by as she wrestled to open them. Finally, too scared to make noise forcing them, and with precious time running away before the Mexican woman came looking for her, she gently raised the window blind so moonlight flooded in and turned her hasty attention to various cabinets that weren't secured.

In a far corner, in a bottom drawer, she found two stout hide saddle-bags that looked familiar. She opened one.

Her heart sang. It was empty except for some twists

of torn paper that proved when taken to the window to be paper bands of the type banks pasted around stacked bills. They were rubber-stamped with the legend 'Ranchers' and Miners' Bank, Silver Vein'.

Proof!

She took one of the bands and hid it away with her Colt and left the office promptly to return to the dormitory.

A sigh of relief was on her lips. So far, it had been easier than she'd dared to expect. She had material evidence after all to bring to the notice of the bank authorities. If she could persuade them to instigate a search of Pickford's, the incriminating saddle-bags and the rest of the paper bands would be found, if not some of the money itself.

But first she had to scat from this place. Again, she might have to call on Lucky's help.

Frustratingly, no opportunity for Lil's escape presented itself for several days. Once she did know about her chance though, she was able to communicate with Lucky in advance when Wal Deegan detailed him to bring out the letters and wire messages that arrived regularly for Dr Guiscard from the East.

Dr Guiscard had scheduled a spectacular mass cure at Arcadia Park.

The Mexicans and Deegan's men were full of it. Tribune Springs was buzzing with interest in the activities of the celebrated French doctor who'd come to live if not exactly in their midst, in close proximity. Deegan was selling high-priced tickets entitling the select holders to view the spectacle of Guiscard treating his patients' maladies.

The occasion was to be a show – an entertainment in the grand tradition of Franz Anton Mesmer, the Viennese father of mesmerism who'd caused a sensation in the salons of Paris at the end of the previous century.

Lil and Lucky had hurried discussions.

'I don't want to become part of the circus,' Lil said, 'but it could be the best time to get me out of the place. Sounds like the visiting audience has been fired up to expect a party.'

Lucky sniggered. 'Mebbe an orgy! 'Fraid a whole lot o' the doc's high-falutin' city ladies are half-locoed. Mebbe the townies'll be a-tryin' to steal kisses!'

'It's not a thing for funning about, Lucky. I've found what I came here for, but getting myself accepted as a patient wasn't as smart as we thought. Suppose Dr Guiscard were to choose me for closer examination. . . .'

'Bah! *That* all's eatin' you? You're worryin' too much, Lil.'

'He'd be sure to recognize me as the girl he made rob a bank for him. How could he forget?'

'You look real diff'rent in women's duds an' with fair hair.'

'Till the dyed stuff starts growing out, and I think it is. My hair's dark again at the roots. Seems now like it was a whole lot easier to get into this ranch than to get out. It's a kind of prison. The whole outfit seems a crazy, lunatic place!'

'Aw, quit frettin', Lil,' Lucky said carelessly. 'Whoever said Pickford's weren't gonna be no madhouse? What we got ain't no bad deal. Thar's time enough. The law'll never find us, an' Deegan ain't such a bad feller.'

'Hmm. To some!'

He grinned at her. 'Sure, he's crooked, but he ain't no Hamish Howard. He works at his rackets. An' he lets his boys git their sport!'

One of Guiscard's Mexicans came out into the yard where they were conferring, ostensibly to dump the contents of a kitchen scrub bucket into the dust. They parted with quiet but abrupt 'so longs', less their parleying should lead to curiosity, arouse suspicion.

Lil stared after Lucky in perplexity and no small measure of concern. She'd become very conscious of her isolation here. She liked wilderness places but Pickford's was a Godforsaken place. Anything could happen to a girl here, and who would be the wiser?

She was pinning her hopes on the unruly Texan playing a key part in the escape plan. There was no one else she could turn to for help.

She had to have complete trust in him.

The nagging question in the back of her mind was, could she?

15

TRUE COLOURS

I don't like this, Misfit Lil told herself. I don't like it at all! I've walked into a trap I set myself, and it's about to go off. . . .

Events were moving rapidly toward a climax for which she was ill-prepared. She felt it in her bones.

The centrepiece for Guiscard's spectacular mass cure was a device he called the *baquet.* It was a big tub made of oak, about a foot deep, which accommodated a dozen people.

The tub had been set up in what had once been the ranch's vast hay barn but was now arranged like a set for a play on a stage. The walls were hung with heavy, dark-red drapes, lit eerily by lanterns which had stained-glass bulls'-eyes and had been fixed high in the roof. The burning of incense completed an atmosphere that was heady, hallucinatory.

Lining the draped walls was a closely packed ring of

spectators, both men and women, policed by Marshal Deegan's deputies, who stood in front of them to prevent any movement forward. The spectators were intent, serious and well behaved, though to Lil's eye some of them looked as though they might have been drinking on the ride out to Pickford's.

They also wore an air of expectancy. Their gaze was fixed on the circle of patients waiting between themselves and the tub. The patients, it had been announced, would take off their robes and be helped into the water by Guiscard's Mexican *femmes de chambre* and Deegan's deputies after the doctor's arrival.

Inside the tub were corked flagons filled with 'magnetized' water, lying on their sides with the necks projecting outward. Water to cover the flagons had been poured into the tub.

The rest of the apparatus for the treatment stood at hand: gunny sacks filled with iron filings, which would be sprinkled into the water, and a sort of cover for the tub with iron rods slotted through it.

It had been explained to the patients, of whom Lil was one, that they would be required to bring the rods in contact with what they considered their 'afflicted parts' while holding hands and pressing their knees against the persons next to them. No one was to speak.

Lil's plan was that Lucky would facilitate her discreet departure during the bustle of the final preparations.

As the moment drew close, a soprano's disembodied voice drifted through Guiscard's improvised salon from what had once been the barn's loft. The voice, singing in Spanish, had a melancholy, ghostly quality.

Around Lil, some of the more suggestible patients began to succumb with hysterical cries to the surrounding strangeness. Lil felt her own heart begin to beat faster. . . .

Her feeling of disquiet mounted.

Then a great door at the end of the barn was flung back and François Guiscard made a theatrical entry in a purple silk gown. Murmurs and gasps ran through the watchers.

Speaking in low tones, Guiscard moved among his patients, making passes with a scintillating crystal wand which became an object of fixation till his dark, mesmerizing eyes caught and held theirs. He attended to them, woman by woman, starting with the most agitated.

It was impressively done. For most, delirium passed and they grew quiet. Only two lost complete control under Guiscard's attentions, and they were carried out by Deegan's men.

Lil's agitation swelled. What was Lucky M'Cline delaying for? Around her women were starting to undress – or be undressed – for immersion in the tub. A low buzz of appreciation was coming from the audience.

Lil was no prude but she found the situation intensely distasteful. The women were 'smooth hides' of a genteel type. Back in their old home environments, they were the kind to blush furiously and leave the room if a gentleman so much as used a 'damn' in conversation. But with free will abandoned, and taking on an alien temperament under the mesmerist's influence, they exposed their bodies, sometimes with help they showed no inclination to resist. One by one, they climbed in a state of nature into the communal tub.

Deegan's men were selecting volunteers from the audience to come forward and assist in the preparations. There was no shortage and a mite of pushing and shoving to be among the chosen. Now was the time for Lucky to help cover her departure, perhaps as one of those embarrassing patients who'd proved uncooperative and who'd been taken away for correction and catharsis out of sight.

Lil manoeuvred herself close to Lucky who seemed to be avoiding her in favour of another woman, a well-developed blonde.

'Come on,' she hissed. 'I'm ready to quit – to fight our way out if we have to!'

Lucky chuckled softly. 'You oughta bin a man, Lil, but I'm most mighty glad you're not! Git your clothes off, jump inta the tub an' lie back an' enjoy it!'

Lil could smell the liquor about him but he was quite sober. She had a sudden sinking sensation in the pit of her stomach. She was afraid.

Her ally and trail partner had abandoned her; this was no playful ribbing by a smart-alec kid. He meant exactly what he said. She sensed that if it became necessary, he'd throw her to Deegan's wolves with no more compunction than an outlaw shooting a stolen horse he'd ridden into the ground.

Despairing and furious, she forced herself to lapse back into a simulated hypnotic trance while Lucky moved away, to hand the busty blonde over the side of the tub.

A plump Mexican woman and Wal Deegan himself closed in on Lil, unknotting the ties of her robe and tugging it open. Resistance was hopeless. Lil gave up modesty to the demands of her predicament. She allowed herself to be divested of the only substantial item she'd been permitted to wear.

'Maria,' Deegan then ordered the Mexican, 'do the honours, *por favor*!'

Lil continued to play possum, putting what she hoped was a vacant, staring look on her face. It was difficult when she hated what was about to be done to her. The instinct of any girl in her right senses was to fight.

Maria's surprisingly nimble-fingered undoing of a few strings set Lil's undergarments loose and their removal was the work of a moment. Her arms were raised and her flimsy chemise pulled over her head; her petticoat fell away and her drawers were whisked to her ankles. She'd not, of course, dared to wear her Colt.

Normally, the bouncing curls of her long dark hair would have left her a minimum of cover, while scarcely reaching her breasts, but when she'd bleached her hair she'd also cropped it. Her exposure felt – and was – total. Trembling with anger and mortification, she let Deegan lift her in powerful arms.

'We got a beauty here!' he said. 'Ain't overmuch fat on her, but she's supple!'

Maria unhooked the drawers hanging loosely from her bare feet, and Deegan deposited her with the other women in the *baquet*.

Across the tub, Lucky was rubbing the blonde's shoulders and back. He had the nerve to wink at Lil.

Several mesmerized women were being subjected to ancillary massage treatment by both the male and female helpers ranked behind them. Hands wandered between the magnetized flagons, seeking out more interesting and sensitive zones hidden in the darkness of the water.

None of the entranced women rejected the attentions.

'Ain't this jest the damnedest frolic yuh ever saw?' a watcher asked quietly.

'Dead right it is,' his neighbour growled back. 'Beats a town dance all holler!'

The combined effects of the sweet, slightly distant notes of the unseen singer, the strange lighting and the drugging incense augmented the efforts of one privileged townie. He succeeded in bringing one young woman, who was an exquisitely white- and freckle-skinned redhead, to a gasping crisis.

Despite his reserved manner, Dr Guiscard was tolerably pleased with the progress of his exhibition. He drew himself up proudly in his fine purple raiment.

'*Voilà*!' he boomed. '*Mademoiselle* is invigorated, refreshed. . . ! Liberated! It is the experience *extatique*.. . .'

'That's exactly what it is, or I'm a liar,' Deegan chortled. 'I figure you folks'll agree it's worth the price of attendance just to witness such natural cures.'

Amid all the distraction Lil saw a slim chance – maybe the only one she'd get. Naked, unarmed and vulnerable, she was desperate enough to take the risk.

Taking advantage of the fascination in the breathless redhead, she leaped from the *baquet* and snatched the surprised Deegan's six-shooter from its holster.

She'd intended to hold it point-blank to the self-serving marshal's head and demand her safe passage to freedom. But it wasn't to work out that way.

Lucky M'Cline was the one person present aware that Lil was an infiltrator with the exposure and destruction of Dr Guiscard and his new boss on her mind. His loyalties were only momentarily divided. He showed his true colours. First and foremost, Lucky was interested in personal gratification. At bottom, fun and continued safety came out tops.

He went for his gun to preserve his new and satisfying situation as a Deegan bully-boy.

Lil's reaction was instinctive. Let down by Lucky, threatened by him, she swung Deegan's gun and shot first. Any pause for cold consideration would have produced the same conclusion: she was in no position to allow him another chance. But she shot without thought. No hesitation, no indecision.

And she didn't shoot to disarm. That was a fancy trick. When you were in a fix as tight as she was, you aimed for the bigger target of body mass. Aimed to stop. Regrettably, that often also meant you killed.

Lucky was hit in the breast. He gave a disbelieving, shocked cry.

Eyes rapidly widening, he jerked, 'Lil! I'm hurt terrible bad!'

He dropped his gun, clasped his hands over the

wound, went down on his knees and keeled over on to his side.

Lil's grey eyes were glistening with moisture, but it was no time to lose her head.

Deegan snatched at her gun arm. Being wet, slippery and totally naked from the tub allowed her to wrench free from his clutching fingers. They had nothing on which to gain purchase.

Eel-like, Lil whipped around and used his revolver again. On him.

At close quarters, the heavy Smith & Wesson's slug ripped through Deegan's thigh, throwing him off his feet and dumping him in the puddles spilled from the tub. Only for seconds did the big blond marshal wriggle about on the wet floor, trying to staunch the fountain of veinous blood pumping from the ragged hole. Then he, too, was still and dead.

That settled it. A few of Deegan's toughs had been reaching for their sidearms, but with the boss and one of their number dead, they changed their minds. Taking advantage of helpless, hysterical women was one thing; duelling with a woman who was hell on wheels with a gun was another.

The panicking townies were already fleeing the barn. The sport had suddenly turned sour and most had sufficient sense to realize that what they'd been participating in wasn't right.

Within moments, the place had emptied, except for Lil and the out-of-it women in the tub.

Then Lil realized Dr Guiscard was also no longer present.

His jig was up, she thought grimly, but she could hazard a guess where he would have gone, before he, too, joined the exodus.

Lil ran the evil mesmerist to earth in the ranch-house office where she'd previously found the saddle-bags that had once contained the Silver Vein bank haul.

He was behind the desk, its drawers unlocked, and he was hastily stuffing the remnants of his loot into a carpetbag.

Lil had paused only to shrug into a robe and Deegan's Smith & Wesson was still gripped in her right fist. She lifted the weapon high and aimed it. Her finger was tight on the trigger.

'You're a thief and a murderer, Dr Guiscard,' she said, 'and you're taking that stuff nowhere except to the nearest honest law office.'

Guiscard laughed in her face.

'You will never get me there!' he mocked. '*Il est comme ceci.* You're a dangerous young woman with a tongue that can be more dangerous still, but one girl cannot go on for ever, and my mental powers are greater than yours.'

'You'll never put me in a trance again!'

'*Non?* Long before you get your way, I will see to it that you run into the trouble you ask for!'

Lil heard the sound of booted feet, approaching at a run. She moved partly aside to cover both Guiscard and the door, not knowing what to expect. Despite her precaution, her surprise was so great when the arrival showed that she momentarily let attention wander from the sneering man she held at gunpoint.

'Jackson!' she blurted. 'Can it be you?'

Jackson Farraday responded with no greeting. He rapped, '*Lil, look out*!'

Lil whirled back to Guiscard. He'd wasted not a split-second in seizing his chance. She was in time to see him bringing up a derringer pistol from the open top drawer of the desk.

The sounds of the exploding Smith & Wesson and the derringer were as one mighty crack of doom that left all ears ringing.

Except Dr Guiscard's.

Lil's aim was sure; his was not. He had a great hole in the centre of his forehead and the back of his skull was blown out, spattering the wall behind him with red and grey blotches.

The smoking Smith & Wesson that had done the horrific damage fell to the office floor with a thud. Impetuously, Lil rushed to Jackson and flung her arms around him.

'Oh, thank God! It is you! How? Why. . . ?'

Weeks of tension and fear ebbed from her. She'd not realized till now just how wound up she'd been.

Jackson Farraday disengaged her gently from him, holding her at arm's length. His calm blue eyes looked into her face, bringing her strength.

'Yes, it is me, Lil Goodnight. The trouble with you, young woman, is that you're so damn self-sufficient but needy at the same time. When I came back to Silver Vein and heard all that had happened, I was unconvinced you'd robbed the bank and killed a teller.

I set out straight away. And what a chase you and Lucky M'Cline have led me!'

Lil heard the reproof in his steady voice, but dare she read significance into his actions?

As though to quash any romantic notions she might be apt to form on account of his long ride, Jackson proceeded in a practical fashion to demand that Lil explain forthwith the queer set-up he'd walked into at Pickford's.

'I want to be told everything about this bizarre Arcadia Park. . . .'

Later, they rounded up two of Dr Guiscard's *femmes de chambre* who hadn't hightailed it with their companions and put them to caring for the semi-comatose women who'd still been languishing in the big tub.

That left only two dead men in the barn.

Lil ignored Marshal Deegan, but she went on her knees beside Lucky. She felt sick inside. In death, nothing was left of the warm, high-spirited Texas kid. A tear rolled down her cheek.

'I wasn't in love with him, like Virginia Whitpath was, but what a terrible waste.'

'Come away, Lil,' Jackson said gruffly. 'We've reports to make and there's nothing more we can do here that can't be done better by other folks . . . territorial authority.'

Lil's eyes came up to him hopefully, wistfully.

'You know something, Jackson. You're always right about official things like that. What do you think? Will they let us ride back to Silver Vein soon? Together?'

Jackson laughed softly.

'Oh, I'm sure they will. But when she can cope with the cleverest charlatans and the biggest and baddest lawmen of this world, does our Misfit Lil need a man to protect her?'

Lil raised a smile. 'Sure she does!'

And she knew he knew that much was true.

It was comforting for her to believe Jackson would always be there when she needed him. Putting her high on his list of priorities. A rock to lean on. No need at this time to talk about those things further.

Her heart was full again with her eternal hope. The person who mattered the most was here to accompany her on the long ride back across the white-tipped purple mountains to home.

Though she knew the hope was vain in critical ways, she vowed silently she'd make the most of their days alone together, riding under a pure blue summer sky, high in the wild Rockies.